THE LAKE

THE
LAKE

BANANA YOSHIMOTO

TRANSLATED BY MICHAEL EMMERICH

MELVILLEHOUSE
BROOKLYN, NEW YORK

The Lake

Originally published by Foil Co., Ltd., in Japanese, as *Mizuumi*

© 2005 by Banana Yoshimoto

Translation © 2011 by Michael Emmerich

First Melville House printing: April 2011

Melville House Publishing

145 Plymouth Street

Brooklyn, NY 11201

www.mhpbooks.com

ISBN: 978-1-933633-77-0

Printed in the United States of America

1 2 3 4 5 6 7 8 9 10

Library of Congress Cataloging-in-Publication

Yoshimoto, Banana, 1964-

[Mizuumi. English]

The lake / by Banana Yoshimoto ; translated by Michael Emmerich.

    p. cm.

ISBN 978-1-933633-77-0

I. Emmerich, Michael. II. Title.

PL865.O7138M5913 2011

895.6'35--dc22

                                        2011006711

The first time Nakajima stayed over, I dreamed of my dead mom.

Maybe it was having him in the room that did it, after having been alone so long.

I hadn't slept next to anyone since my dad and I stayed in my mom's hospital room.

I kept waking up and then, relieved that she hadn't stopped breathing, going back to sleep. The floor was dustier than you'd expect in a hospital, and I lay staring at a ball of lint that was always in exactly the same place. I didn't sleep well, and whenever I drifted into wakefulness I would hear the footsteps of nurses moving down the hallway. And it occurred to me that I was surrounded by people who could die at any minute, and in some odd way their presence made me feel more at ease here, in the hospital, than I did outside.

When things get really bad, you take comfort in the *placeness* of a place.

I hadn't dreamed of my mom since she died.

Or rather, sometimes she would appear in disconnected fragments of dream as I drifted off to sleep, but until that night she had never been there so clearly or for so long. Somehow I had the feeling, when I awoke, that I had been with her again, for real, after a very long separation.

That's an odd thing to say about someone who's dead, but that's how it felt.

You could almost say my mom had two different faces. Two selves that came and went inside her, went and came, like distinct personalities.

One was sociable and upbeat, a woman of the world who lived in the moment and seemed like a really cool person to be around; the other was extremely delicate, like a big, soft flower nodding gently on its stem, looking as if the slightest breeze would scatter its petals.

The flowerlike side wasn't easy to recognize, and my mom, always eager to please, tried hard to cultivate the feisty, easygoing side of her personality. Watering it, rather than the flower, with lots of love, fertilizing it with people's approval.

My mom wasn't married to my dad when she had me.

My dad was the president of a small import-export company in a large town on the outskirts of Tokyo, and my mom was the reasonably beautiful owner, the "Mama-san," of a ritzy club in the entertainment district of that same town.

One night, a business associate invited my dad out drinking and took him to my mom's club. My dad fell for my mom the moment he set eyes on her. She had a good feeling about him, too. When it came time to close up shop, they went to a Korean restaurant and ordered all sorts of dishes, laughing like crazy and having a ball, sharing their food like old friends. My dad went back to the club the next night, and the next, and so on, even when it had snowed—he went so often that in two months they were a couple. Considering how they met, two months seems like a pretty long time. That's what makes it seem like the real thing.

They always gave the same answer when I asked what made them laugh so hard.

"Because it was a restaurant with no Japanese customers, just a place we'd stumbled across, wandering around in the middle of the night. And since we couldn't read the menu, we ended up ordering a whole bunch of things at random, and the waiter kept carting out one dish after another, foods we didn't recognize at all, some of them incredibly spicy, and the portions were much bigger than we had expected ... it was hilarious."

I don't buy it, though.

I think they were just so happy to be sitting across the table from each other that night that the excitement made them giddy. I'm sure they had to endure all kinds of social pressure, but in front of me they were always very sweet to each other. They used to quarrel all the time, it's true, but even that was kind of cute—like little kids having an argument.

My mom really wanted a baby, and she got pregnant with me immediately; but even then my parents never officially married. It wasn't the usual story, though. My dad didn't already have a wife and family, and he doesn't have anyone else now.

His relatives were the problem. They were dead set against the union, and my dad didn't want to drag my mom into a fight. So I grew up as an acknowledged but illegitimate child.

You hear a lot of talk about families like ours. In the end, though, my dad was home more than he was away, and I wasn't miserable at all.

Except for being totally sick of that environment.

Sick of the town, sick of the situation, sick of everything. I was dying to get away from it all. I could almost convince myself it was a good thing my mom had died, because now I would never, ever have to go back there. Except for the fact that I no longer saw my dad as much as I used to, I didn't regret anything. He had already sold the apartment where my mom and I used to live, to keep it from becoming the epicenter of an all-out dogfight among his relatives, and he'd put the money in my bank account. I felt like I was being awarded damages for her death or something, and I didn't like that; but on the other hand, the cash was my inheritance from her. And that was all I needed to be free. There was nothing left in my old hometown now to show that I had ever been there. I couldn't say that made me sad, though.

Take my mom's club, for instance: When you went in during the daytime, the place looked dark and a little dingy, and it stank faintly of alcohol and cigarettes. I felt utterly, totally blank there. And when my mom's flashy outfits came back from the cleaners and I saw them in the daylight, they seemed so cheap and flimsy it was pathetic.

All those emotions, balled up, were how I felt about the town.

It's no different, even now that I'm going on thirty.

Last time I saw my dad, he stared at me with moist eyes.

I've come to resemble her.

"It's such a waste—the best times of our life were still to come. We were looking forward to old age, relaxing, traveling together. We were planning to go on a round-the-world cruise. If I'd known things would end this way, we could have gone and done all that stuff instead of making excuses about my job, about how your mother couldn't spare the time, couldn't afford to leave the club."

I'm sure my dad must have played around when he was younger, since he could hold his liquor and loved to socialize, but as far as I know he was never seriously involved with another woman after he and my mom got together.

My dad has this notion that he has to come across as a playboy, and even though he tries to act the role, it's obvious that it's just a pose. He's the sort of guy who looks like a dweeb no matter what he does—and what's more, he's the perfect image of a balding, middle-aged hick. There's nothing even remotely sexy about him. He's totally uncool. So earnest that a real, bona-fide playboy would burst out laughing at the sight of him.

At heart my dad is an uncomplicated guy, but his position, the need to take over his father's business, put a lot of strain on him, and he never seems to have felt any desire to break out of that. So he's muddled through life, going through the motions, doing whatever it takes to fit into a recognizable mold. The son of a rich, land-owning family. The president of an import-export company in a provincial town. That, at any rate, is my take on him.

I guess my mom was all he had—the one flower that smelled like freedom.

He was careful never to let outside business intrude on the spaces he shared with my mom. He made it seem like the man he was at home was who he really wanted to be. Whenever he came to spend time with us, he threw himself into household tasks: fixing the roof, puttering in the garden, going out to eat with my mom, checking my homework, tuning up my bike.

My parents never even considered leaving town to try and find a lifestyle that was actually their own. Because being there together, hemmed in—that *was* their way of life.

I think now my dad is afraid, more than anything, that I'll abandon him.

He's not really afraid. He just thinks about it, with a shiver.

He wonders if one day I'll tell him: *We never had the same family name anyway, so starting today, that's how it's going to be. I don't want anything more to do with you.*

Sometimes, for no reason, he puts money in my bank account or mails me food. I call to say thank you. His nervousness is palpable, radiating from the receiver.

I know what he's thinking: *We're still father and daughter, right? Right?*

I thank him, and I accept the money, but I've never told him in so many words that our relationship will go on like this, like a real family, because I don't feel I need to. That's not the kind of relationship we have: he'll always be my dad, whatever anxieties the little prickings of his conscience may inspire in him, and even if I did try to abandon him.

Unlike my dad, I don't have to worry about these things.

I wouldn't be unwilling to lean on him for support if the need arose, but at the same time I know that if I let him give me anything too solid, too permanent, certain people out there who are driven by a jealousy and a desire I can't fathom would come swooping in around me, eager to inspect it. It's totally clear to me that all they're after are the pleasures of voyeurism, but still it'd be a pain in the ass to have to deal with them.

Everything that tied me to my hometown was a pain. The less of it the better.

I know my parents had their own ideas, but from my perspective their feet were shackled and the chains bound them to my hometown.

All my life, I cherished the possibility of escape. I worried that if I started going out with a guy and somehow botched things up and fell seriously in love, if we ended up having a splendid wedding in some hotel in town—or even worse, if I happened to get pregnant!—well, that would be the end of everything. So while my classmates thrilled over their puppy loves and fantasized about getting married, I held myself back. Before I did anything, I considered the possible consequences. And as soon as I graduated from high school, on the pretext of attending an art school in Tokyo, I made my getaway. I left home.

My body knew. It sensed the discrimination, subtle but real, all around me.

Sure, she's the daughter of a prominent local figure, but c'mon—he knocked up the Mama-san of a bar, right? That's the kind of girl she is. The feeling oppressed me, squeezing all the more tightly because I knew it was only in this city, nowhere else, that my dad mattered.

When I came to Tokyo and became an ordinary art school student, just like everyone else, I felt so free and light I thought I'd float up into the air.

I remember how I felt when my father's relatives came to see my mom laid out in her coffin, everyone overcome with curiosity, fascinated by her, jealous of her, putting on a show in their obligatory black mourning suits and dresses and kimono, all made up in their phony solemnity, their faces full of grief but their eyes shining, biting into her ... I wanted to strip and dance naked in front of them, because maybe then I could have demolished the fake, slimy atmosphere they had created. As long as I live, I'll never forget that feeling.

But the mourners' dirty stares couldn't touch my mom's body: her corpse was eased into the flames and made pure. I hadn't realized her cremation would bring me such relief. I could see that their curiosity was perfectly well satisfied by the clothes my mom was wearing, by her ordinary good looks, and by the intensity with which my dad had prepared a funeral that was, in the end, magnificent, and for which no expense had been spared.

It was my duty to lead the ceremony, so I made a speech, I smiled at people, and every so often I shed a tear and dabbed at it, just for show; but inside, I was raging, quivering with a sense of indignation that I couldn't communicate to anyone.

My fury was lofty, pure, cool. It was an emotion that none of these people, struggling so hard to impose a shape on a life when life has no shape, could begin to understand.

I was grateful, though, despite everything, when one middle-aged woman who lived nearby and my mom's few friends reached out to me; I had some good moments with them, and we shared a few cups of steaming tea. Everything in life has some good in it. And when something awful happens, the goodness stands out even more—it's sad, but that's the truth. The women didn't have to say it, because their eyes did: *We know, darling, we know you're hurting.*

And yet . . . when I saw my dad clinging to the coffin, sobbing and wailing, I knew that I had gotten the short end of the stick in all this. My dad wasn't paying the slightest attention to anyone but her, and here I was getting miffed about things that were totally pointless.

Standing there, a witness to the end of the century's

greatest romance (even if my parents were the only ones who saw it that way), I was just a little girl, trembling at the death of a parent. Of course, maybe that's only to be expected. A husband is different from a daughter.

At any rate ... when my mom appeared in my dream that night, it was the flowerlike her, not the other one.

The mom I really wanted to see, who seemed to be peeking out bashfully from underneath an umbrella of thin, fluttering petals.

She spoke to me. We were in the hospital room where she had lived out her last days. She hadn't sat up in the longest time, so when I saw her doing that in my dream, leaning against the headboard, I couldn't help feeling nostalgic.

A breeze blew in through the open window, making the sunlight churn brilliantly in the air, and in her pink pajamas my mom looked just like a high school girl on an overnight class trip. She was enveloped in a sort of beautiful haze. The flowers her visitors had brought seemed like they were about to dissolve into her light.

She was too dazzling to look at straight on, so I fixed my gaze on the film of dust that had accumulated on the windowsill.

My mom spoke to me.

"You know, Chihiro, darling—all it takes is one little wrong step and you end up feeling frustrated your whole life, like me. If you're always angry, always yelling at people, ultimately that just means you depend on them."

I know, I thought, I know. You weren't really the sort to nag at people, to fawn over your regular customers to protect your business, or to snap at Dad over the phone when he was too busy to come see us; you weren't the kind of person to grumble, at such times, *What right do I have to complain? I'm just your partner, after all, not a* real *wife*. Your outlook wasn't so jaded ... the truth is, Mom, you weren't even a wildflower blooming in a field, as they say, you were such an extraordinarily delicate, transparent person that, if anything, you were like a blossom softly unfurling its petals on a cliff somewhere, so high that no one ever came your way, no one but birds and deer ... I know, I thought, I know.

Dad knew, too. He understood, the best he could, and watched over you.

Because when you were relaxing with him, you always looked like a little girl. You were like children, both of you. Only society, the world at large, wouldn't let you be.

I guess you just lacked the courage, the guts to strike out on your own. And so when it all came to an end, you were still living that way, a life you never meant to be anything more than a stopgap, filling in for the real thing.

These were all just thoughts running through my mind,

but of course these things are easy in dreams. My mom nodded. And then she continued.

"I didn't want things to be that way. I never really liked
makeup, either. I hated the idea of having plastic surgery
done so I'd look young again, I was terrified of the surgeon,
and I was frightened of seeing people there, at the surgeon's,
who wanted to be beautiful. In one way or another, I was
always in pain, always scared. But when people told me I
should do something, I started to think that maybe I had to,
and so I would—it was as simple as that. And once I'd done
it, it was done, and I had to cover up how scared it made me,
so I'd turn it all into a joke, even though deep down inside
my heart was aching.

"Of course I didn't want to be always griping at your dad.
But I worried constantly that he might drift away from me,
so I clung to him as hard as I could. I knew there were other
ways, besides anger, to show what I was feeling, but the anger just came. Somehow I'd ended up on this path, instead
of some other, and it turned out that on this path there was
no turning back. Being anxious only made me more anxious,
and play-acting got a better response, so that was how it had
to be. I couldn't stop myself. In the end, I died before anything could change.

"But you know, Chihiro, from where I am now I can look
out over it all, and I understand much better, I understand
a lot. I see so clearly now that a lot of what happened—it's

not that I'm regretting those things, it's not that—but I didn't really need to worry so much," my mom said. "You see what I mean?"

From where I am now ... Is it heaven? Is heaven real, then? I thought.

My mom smiled vaguely. And she went on.

"I was frightened of so many things, in my vanity, that ultimately I couldn't protect myself any other way. Try not to be like that, okay? Be sure to keep your tummy warm, try to relax, both your heart and your body, try not to get flustered. Live like a flower. You have that right. It's something you can achieve, for sure, in your lifetime. And that's enough."

My mom smiled brightly, and all of a sudden I remembered how, when I was little, I used to push the blanket off my stomach when I slept, and when my mom came in to check on me she would tell me to keep my tummy warm. Even in my dream, tears came to my eyes.

All throughout my childhood, whenever my eyes fluttered open at night, my mom would be there, giving my bare stomach a gentle pat, rearranging my pajamas, spreading the blanket over me. How many times had I seen her do this?

This is what it means to be loved ... when someone wants to touch you, to be tender ... My body still remembers that feeling, even now. My body knows not to respond to fake love. I guess maybe that's what it means to have been brought up well.

Mom, let me see you once more, I prayed. *I want to touch you. To smell your smell.*

I miss even the club, in all its daylight dinginess, now that I know it's gone.

Maybe it wasn't the most gorgeous place, but that's where I come from. That world had my mom's smell. In the end, I know it was as comforting to me as it was oppressive. I'm still a child, I still need my parents, and yet, suddenly, I find that I am walking alone.

In my dream, I felt twice as sad and so weak it almost crushed me.

Tears were trickling down my cheeks when I woke.

Waking up with a start, I glanced over at Nakajima, who was lying beside me on a futon of his own, sound asleep. He had pushed his arm out from under the covers, and it looked cold, lying there on the tatami. I gave the comforter a tug, pulling it up over him.

Now that I was back in the real world, the dream didn't seem so sad. The sense of my mom, of her presence, kept radiating warmly through my chest, though I still didn't feel any affection for the town where I'd grown up.

Why, I wondered, had I suddenly gone back to being a child again? Probably somewhere deep down, a part of me was still holding on to the past, just a little...

I was *here* enough now, though, to analyze my emotions.

- *The one thing I kind of miss is the apartment, now that it's not ours anymore. Sometimes I wish I could go back and live there again, and go back to being a child...*

I cast my memory back.

The cheerful mood on Sunday mornings—the sounds of programs more fun and easygoing than anything on TV today streaming into the room as my dad sat taking it easy, waiting for what would be breakfast and lunch combined, while in the kitchen my mom experimented with a palette of imported ingredients, mixing up some sort of ethnic dish.... They were both slightly hungover from the night before, and looking back now I realize that something of the tender lethargy that follows sex hung in the air. Their languor made them seem so gentle, so sleepy. I used to lie in bed as a child, gazing out at that world, entranced.

I wouldn't mind going back to my hometown as it was then.

And then, once again, I noticed with a start that Nakajima was lying beside me. That's odd. What's he doing here? If this is a dream, don't let me wake up.

Right, I remember. He decided to spend the night.

Slowly my memory began to kick in.

I found myself recalling, without exactly meaning to, the earnest sexual exchange we had bumbled through before we fell asleep, and I felt a bit embarrassed. Now we had our pajamas on, lying on our separate futons, as if nothing had happened. It was as though we had been living together for ages, and yet Nakajima's presence still came as a shock. I felt somewhat bewildered, somewhat calm, somewhat giddy. Maybe that's why I had dreamed of my mom.

I don't often get to spend time with such an unusual guy.

For some reason I had made up my mind that Nakajima wouldn't want to stay in the same room with anyone else for long. I had seen him in his apartment with a woman I assumed was his girlfriend, but I didn't get the sense that they were always together.

The night before, Nakajima had told me tearfully that he was afraid if he let this chance go, he'd never be able to have sex with anyone for the rest of his life. Oh please, I had said, you're exaggerating. At the same time, imagining what it took for him to confess something like that, I started to feel a bit sorry for him, and I got sad myself. My mood grew somber.

And then what happened? Did we go all the way? Or not?

We hadn't been drinking, and yet I could remember only fragments of what had happened. Whatever, I thought, who cares. He's still here.

Again the sense of my mom's presence wafted through my mind.

That was a sad dream, I thought. But it was beautiful.

My mom was really there—the mom I wanted to see, who came so rarely.

She always spoke her mind, she could laugh anything off, she was proud, and she made you feel that you could lean on her as much as you liked, it didn't bother her, so eventually even I began to forget her true nature, which that façade concealed.

But when I was little—on certain rare occasions when she smiled at me with a special, airy softness, or when we warmed our cold feet against each other in the futon we shared, or when we set out on an exhilarating walk the morning after a snowfall, leaving a line of footprints in the freshly fallen snow ... at such times, her true self would surface, she was like a little girl, and it seemed as if she would stay that way forever.

I stared blankly at Nakajima's chest as I relived these memories, watching it rise and fall, and little by little I began to feel calmer, as if I were succumbing to hypnosis.

Nakajima. Nakajima ... funny-looking Nakajima.

Those pinched nostrils, his stick-thin wrists and long fingers, the way his mouth gaped as he slept, the almost touching scrawniness of his neck, the childish fullness of his cheeks, and the way his smooth hair tumbled over his eyes, so that his narrow eyes themselves, with their long eyelashes, seemed to be hiding ... I adored it all, everything about him. I found myself thinking that when, far in the future, Nakajima heaves his final breath and floats up into the sky to take his place among the stars (I know I've heard that metaphor before, but it seems to fit him so perfectly—in fact, the image of him becoming a star is almost *too* appropriate, considering how weak a hold life seems to have on him), my spirit will be with him. What I felt for him wasn't exactly love, it was closer to a sense of surprise, even shock. And so I just kept watching him, unable to get completely involved.

He's still here today, I thought. *He hasn't disappeared. And I still feel the same way!*

Each day was so fresh, now that I had become hopelessly attracted to this puzzling young man, Nakajima. Ever since we started hanging out, I'd been out of sorts. For years now I had been thinking only of myself, struggling to get my own way, pressing relentlessly forward, my gaze trained on an ideal future—I'd been focused exclusively on putting as much distance as I could between me and my hometown, steadfastly refusing to put down roots. But Nakajima was so intense he had rolled right over me, and now he was dragging me along behind him.

Here, time didn't exist. We were cut off from rest of the world. Just being with Nakajima made me feel as if we were detached from history, and had no particular age.

Sometimes I even wondered if what I was feeling was happiness.

Time has stopped, and I'm looking at Nakajima, and that's all I want.

Yes, I felt, this must be what it's like to be happy.

I've lived an utterly ordinary life. Well, maybe not—I guess in a town out in the middle of nowhere, where just about anything provides fodder for gossip, being an illegitimate child was enough to make me extraordinary. But there's nothing unusual about me as a person.

So I can't deny that Nakajima—who *is* rather odd—was sometimes a bit too much for me, and in my dealings with him, part of me was always ready to run away.

All I knew about his past was that he had been through something terrible. We had never talked in any depth about what it was.

Nakajima had adored his mother, but he said she had died, and whenever he talked about her he cried. Though I didn't know the details, I could see he had been raised in a way that let him love her like that, openly and honestly; his heart, at least, was in the right place.

And I could see that no one else in the world would ever be able to love him the way his mother must have loved him.

I doubted I had the strength to deal with anything too awful, but somehow that realization seemed to make it easier for me to be around him.

I'm not sure how long it took before Nakajima began staying over. At least a year.

At some point, quite naturally, without either of us

experiencing any big surge of excitement, he started coming to my apartment in the evenings.

He'd drop by whenever I was there, and then when he felt the time had come, late at night, he would go home. Things probably continued like that, one unremarkable visit after the next, for a total of about three months, though I can't say for sure.

It wasn't at all like we were living together. It was more like being roommates. We had our own rooms, they just happened to be a bit farther apart than usual. Nakajima's presence didn't put any pressure on me, either. Quite the reverse: there was a warmth in the core of my chest when he was around. And that feeling stayed.

When all this got started, I was living here in my own apartment, and Nakajima lived on the second floor of the building diagonally across from mine.

I had a habit of standing at my window, looking out, and so did Nakajima, so we noticed each other, and before long we started exchanging nods. I guess it must have been pretty rare in a busy city like Tokyo for two people in two windows to nod to each other when their eyes met, but where I come from, out in the boonies, that was the most natural thing in the world, and Nakajima isn't the sort of person to bother about such things. There's a tenacity in him that's beyond all that. The intensity of a person unafraid of death, at the end of his rope.

Maybe that's how I knew we would get along.

That and the lankiness of his silhouette against the window, and the fact that it made such a perfect picture. Sometimes he let his scrawny arm dangle down over the sill, and I thought he looked wonderful when he did that, like a wild monkey.

As time passed, I started opening my window when I woke up in the morning and glancing over at Nakajima's. I didn't care whether I had gotten dressed, or what state my hair was in or anything—it didn't matter. I felt close to him, and I'd come to regard him as just another part of the scenery. For some reason I was convinced our paths would never actually cross.

Even if I didn't see Nakajima, I'd see his carefully hung-out laundry (he hung it so neatly it was practically an art form. I bet he could have worn his clothes straight off the line, without even ironing them. Compared to him, I was so slovenly I might as well have just bunched mine up and tossed them on the veranda), and every so often I'd see a woman who was clearly older than Nakajima lounging around near the window, and I'd think *Ah, his girlfriend spent the night. Good for him.*

Little by little, an inch at a time, the distance between us narrowed.

I always like to be near the window, no matter how cold it gets, so even during the winter, he and I were constantly waving to each other.

"How are you today?" I'd say.

"I'm okay!" I couldn't hear his voice, but I could read his lips.

And he would smile.

It was as if living where we did had imposed a special destiny on us, giving us feelings that no one else could share. Day after day, we always kept an eye on each other's windows, and so it felt almost as if we were living together. When Nakajima's lights went out, I'd start to think that maybe it was time for me to hit the sack, too, and whenever I came back after a trip home and opened my window, Nakajima would lean out his and shout, "Welcome back!"

Neither of us realized what was happening. That simply by keeping an eye on each other, without even giving it any thought, just by noticing the sound of a certain window sliding open, we were already starting to fall in love.

Eventually, as I accompanied my mom down the long, long path she was headed down, making the trip back and forth from my apartment to my hometown again and again, I found myself taking as much comfort in the glow of Nakajima's window as I did in returning to my own apartment. During those heartbreaking days, that was all the happiness I had.

The time I spent with my dad and my dying mom in that other place left me with plenty of warm memories, it's true, but the moment I stepped from the dark station platform into the train that would carry me back to my apartment, I would be alone. My mom's only child, alone.

I had to make this journey by myself.

As I stood there on the platform, the hard reality of my mom's imminent death would fuse with my memories of her, and with the air of boredom that clung to the people around me as they went about their ordinary lives—everything bled together, and I felt lost. I had no idea where I belonged, whether I was an adult or a child, where my home was, where my roots were. My head began to swim.

I was so agonized, I couldn't even think, *Why don't you fall in love with Nakajima, then? Let him be more of a comfort. Go on, put yourself in his hands! Wouldn't it be nice to see that figure in the window up close?* No, it never even occurred to me.

And yet he was there, in exactly the right place, when I needed him. I'm convinced it would never have worked out if he had been any closer than he was, or any farther away.

Our windows were pretty far apart, with a street running between them, but I didn't feel the distance at all. We seemed, somehow, to be connected. It can't have been that easy for us to hear each other over the voices of passersby and the noise of traffic, but I seemed to have uncannily little trouble making out what he was saying. The sight of his pale face hovering dimly in the darkness, a carefree smile on his lips, made me feel better than anything.

I didn't go out of my way to tell Nakajima when my mom died.

He and I used to go for tea sometimes if we met on the street, and that was what happened when I finally returned from the funeral. I hadn't been home for three weeks, so I cleaned the apartment and then went out to buy groceries; I ran into Nakajima on the way. We went into Starbucks, found two seats at the counter by the window, and sat down with our drinks.

The hubbub of the place and the scent of coffee and the voices of so many young people left me feeling a bit dazed, since I had been away from these things for a while. It occurred to me that if I were a ghost, this ambience was what I'd miss most: the ordinary, day-to-day bustle of the living. Ghosts long, I'm sure, for the stupidest, most unremarkable things.

"I won't have to spend weekends away anymore," I said. "I have hardly any family left in my hometown now, so I'll just go for the occasional visit."

Nakajima took a sip of his coffee, frowning at its heat.

"Your mother died?" he said.

I was taken aback. "How did you know?"

"You've been going back so often lately that, well, I kind of…"

His answer didn't explain anything. I guess he noticed how out of it I've been, I thought, that clued him in. Nakajima picks up on these things. My reflection in the window looked a lot smaller than usual. I looked kind of wilted, fuzzy around the edges. Maybe if you knew what to look for, you could tell at a glance that I had lost a parent.

"I won't be lonely on the weekends, then. I shouldn't say this, I know, but I'm glad. I mean, it was so dull without you, last week, and the week before that, with your window totally dark. You have the nicest window, you know? None of the others can even compete. It's not flashy like the others, or bleary—your window gives off this nice, quiet light."

"Really?"

I wasn't sure I liked being told that it was good my mother had died, but I'd been subjected to so many formulaic expressions of shared grief in the past weeks that I was kind of touched by his honesty.

"I mean it. When your light is out, Chihiro, I feel so alone I can hardly bear it."

Whenever Nakajima said my name, every single time, it sparkled like a treasure. I had no idea why. *Wow—did you see how that flashed? Say it again for me, please!*

Only I couldn't tell him that, so I simply replayed his voice, speaking my name, within me. Something in his tone made me feel, for the first time, a sexy thrill in being with him; but that wasn't all—for some reason, it also made me feel proud.

"I guess it's good I came back, then, huh?"

I couldn't suppress my tears as I said this; I cried a little.

"I know, it hurts when your mom dies," Nakajima said. "It was hard for me, too."

Not knowing much about his background, I simply thought:

So he doesn't have a mother, either.

"Yeah." I sniffled. "But it's a road we all have to walk, right?"

I squeezed the big cup of chai between my hands as if I were hugging it to me, clinging to it. And then, the very next moment, all the things I'd had to confront in such a short space of time, and the fear that maybe I no longer really had a home or a family to go back to—all that lifted, just a little, and I felt free, at ease.

About two weekends later, Nakajima started coming over. It wasn't a big deal, he just came. One second, it seemed, he was in that window, and then the next he was in mine. So I didn't even feel the need to rethink our relationship.

We had run into each other in the street earlier, just like always, when he asked:

"By the way, Chihiro, do you have a boyfriend?"

"Not anymore," I replied. "I was dating this busy editor who only had weekends free, and after I started caring for my mother we never had time to get together, so he dumped me."

"Ah. The bozo didn't like it that your mom was more important."

His use of the word "bozo" made me grin.

Everything he did was adorable. I always saw the best in him. We'd taken our time turning toward each other, from our two windows, piling each little moment on the next until, deep in our hearts, something clicked. And so the surface remained unruffled.

"Yeah, I think that was it," I replied. "So it was kind of hard to care. Trying to make time to see him would have been much, much harder on me. I guess it was kind of a relief to see the last of him. Because more than anything, I really needed time alone—that and some serious sleep."

"I know what you mean..." Nakajima nodded.

He had a habit of frowning slightly when he nodded.

That same night, he started coming to my place to hang out.

We took to doing things together: eating dinner, going out for *yakiniku* at a neighborhood bar (neither of us, especially Nakajima, liked eating out, and we never went drinking), taking turns having baths and cracking beers when we got out, sitting together without talking.

It was odd, but somehow my apartment seemed brighter when Nakajima was there. For the first time in my life, I felt that I had a real friend, and that I wasn't alone.

At some point, I had decided that Nakajima was gay, and the woman who sometimes came to stay with him was just a friend, and that he had his own means of taking care of whatever urges he had, out in the city somewhere.

I got the sense that he wasn't really into sex, and he was shockingly thin, and although there were days when he would consume an astonishing amount, ordinarily he ate almost nothing, so overall he didn't seem very energetic. There was that woman who came over, of course, but they didn't really seem to be involved, and I assumed that on the rare nights when he went out, he headed to a part of town where guys like him gathered.

Or maybe it was my pride that made me want to believe that. Because he seemed so totally uninterested in me. Like I could get dressed in front of him and he wouldn't even blush.

Then last night, Nakajima really, really hadn't wanted to go home.

He kept delaying, trotting out so many excuses that I made a joke of it.

"What, are the debt collectors coming? An old girlfriend?"

"I kind of think something bad happened to me on this day of the year, a long time ago—I feel really uneasy," Nakajima said. "I've got a weirdly precise memory, mentally and physically, and I never do well on the anniversary of a bad day. I'm sorry, though, I can't tell you about what happened right now. I'll get even more agitated if I remember the details."

I was tempted to point out how self-centered he was being, seeing as it was my apartment and he was the one who had come over. But Nakajima looked like he was really hurting, and I got the sense that whatever the story was it was pretty heavy, so I decided not to press him.

I just asked if he wanted to stay over, and he nodded, and that was that.

We left the lights on after we lay the futons out. I read a book, and Nakajima asked if he could watch some movie on TV, and watched it, and for a very long time neither one of us spoke. When the movie ended and Nakajima turned off the TV, I decided maybe it was time to go to bed, and I had just closed my book, thinking how nice it was to have someone else in the room, how reassuring it was to hear him doing this and that, when he spoke.

"Actually, it's not easy for me to have sex."

He was gazing up at the ceiling.

"Ahh ... really?" I said.

I felt a light tremor of surprise, as if he had confessed that he loved me. I'd assumed he was intentionally avoiding that topic.

Just then, I was still dealing with the discovery that when someone important to you dies, you stop having sexual desires. It's like all the water in your body has dried up. That's how it was for me. So if Nakajima had been all slick and eager, I probably would have thrown him out on his ear. I too had been trying, casually, to steer clear of that kind of talk, that mood.

At the same time, I was afraid it would be worse if I lost him now, over this.

I was so worn down from taking care of my mother that I doubted I'd feel like sleeping with anyone anytime soon.

And I'd seen nothing but butts and bedpans and urine bottles, day in and day out; that might have had something to do with it, too. I'd had so much time to myself at the hospital, while my mom was getting tests done, that sometimes I even took care of the old man in the next bed.

I was kind of tired, I guess, of knowing that people are flesh. Flesh and water.

When I changed my mom's pajamas, a smell that you could only describe as the smell of water came wafting up from under her collar. I miss it now, and wish I could smell it again; I wish I could go back to that moment and keep inhaling that smell forever—but at the time it made me think, *God, it's true, people are made of water*, and the thought depressed me.

I hadn't told Nakajima this, but the real reason I'd broken up with my boyfriend was that he kept pushing me to have sex and I kept refusing.

He was so busy with work that we could only really spend time together on Saturdays, if then, so he ended up dropping in on weekday nights, or on Sunday evening. And we would end up in bed, of course. But there was no way, just no way I could get myself into it. As it happened, this guy was bursting with energy, raring to go, morning and night, no matter where we were. That's nice when you're feeling good, but it's not nice at all when you've got other things on your mind. In other words, I really didn't like this guy. He was a sort of sex buddy, and when I first met him it just happened that that's what I wanted. In the excitement of our new relationship, I'd mistaken my eagerness for affection. I thought it was him I wanted.

All along, I didn't realize what had happened, and then one day it hit me. I noticed that I never felt like opening the curtains when he was over, and that clued me in.

I didn't want Nakajima to see him relaxing in my apartment.

When it's like that, no matter who it is, it's clearly not going to work.

On the other hand, here I was with Nakajima—a guy I really did like—hanging around all the time, and still I couldn't do it because I didn't feel happy enough. Even I found it puzzling. Here I had this young guy I liked in front of me, and I wasn't holding back, I just didn't feel turned on. Needless to say, I wasn't thinking at all about how Nakajima might be feeling.

At most, I had a vague sense that maybe someday I'd fall for him.

It's hard to imagine, I know, but Nakajima had this particular aura about him that made it easy to accept anything, and when I luxuriated in that aura, even the most bizarre things came to seem perfectly ordinary.

For instance, after I started spending time with Nakajima, I became clearly aware, for the first time in my life, of the way I had always looked at the world, and of how I wanted to see it in the future. It was because he was so steadfast. All the matters in which I'd let myself flip-flop, changing from day to day, all the times I'd tried to make myself into something I wasn't in order to assuage little stabs of conscience—bitter thoughts about my parents' relationship, say, or how my mother was living her life ... I saw it all so clearly. I'd always felt bad, somewhere in my heart, about my inability to sympathize with my mom, who had tried in her own wishy-washy way to accommodate herself to society, and remained like that until she died. Of course you have to sympathize with her—she was weak, she was only human. Out in the country, people aren't as tough as they are in the city. Living alone in Tokyo as I do now, I'm starting to forget what it's like, but in the countryside those social connections still matter, and that's the world Mom belonged to ... *See how arrogant you are?* I had told myself. *You've got to change that.* And I'd believed it.

But after I met Nakajima and saw how he dove into each day, though only doing the bare minimum, only what he liked, I realized that I was exactly like my mother—the way she tried to be what others wanted her to be, because she was afraid to be different. I had that same fawning impulse, too.

And when it occurred to me that being that way really wasn't going to help me get through the rest of my life, I realized that from now on, my mom's life and mine would have to be completely, unmistakably different. Nothing about us was the same: the times we lived in, the ways we regarded the world, the things we valued. That wasn't to say I didn't love my mom, or that I couldn't respect or forgive her. That's not what I mean.

Tremulously peeling back that film of false sympathy, I discovered a smooth new willingness to let bygones be bygones forming like new skin underneath.

Something flashed in my mind when I discovered that feeling inside me: *So this is what it means to grow up.* And I realized, rather late, that Nakajima, who had been on his own for ages, had also been an adult for a very long time.

And not just an adult: frail as he seemed, he was also a man.

"So if I'm like this, Chihiro, it's not because you're not attractive. I'm sorry."

Nakajima peered awkwardly at me in the dimly lit room as he said this.

"You don't have to apologize. Besides, who said I *want* you to do anything? How do you know what I'm feeling?" I said.

"What? I thought women were like that," Nakajima said. "They always get angry if I don't try to come on to them after a while, once we get friendly."

"I'm not angry yet. Besides, we're kind of still in the process of getting friendly, or maybe that's not quite right, I don't know. I guess I hadn't really thought about it," I said. "So relax."

"Okay. It's just that all kinds of things happened to me. A long time ago. And so it's like, that kind of stuff, it scares me so much, really, I hate it so much I shudder just thinking about it. Getting naked with people and stuff. People being naked. I'm so scared I can't even go to a public bath or a hot springs or anything—do you believe me?" Nakajima said.

I had no idea what had happened, but clearly it was pretty serious.

When someone tells you something big, it's like you're taking money from them, and there's no way it will ever go back to being the way it was. You have to take responsibility for listening.

My mother used to say that. What a stingy way to look at the world, I thought, and yet at the same time I realized it was probably true.

So I'd gotten into the habit of withdrawing into myself whenever people tried to talk.

When you've got a parent who works in a club, you learn very early that the sky's the limit when it comes to terrible stories. Whenever a girl I got to know at school came and launched into some sad tale with a "I don't like to talk about it, but...," it all seemed totally trivial to me. I guess you could say I was mature for my years, at least in terms of the stories I'd heard.

I was still very young, too, when I learned that on some level, whether or not two people had slept together really wasn't such a big deal.

"It's okay, you don't need to tell me. Especially if it hurts," I said. "If I should happen to start feeling that way for you and you still can't perform, I'll just go on out and find another boyfriend and chase you out of here. I won't give you another thought, really. So don't worry about it, okay? It's not a problem. Right now, I'm not in the mood, either. I mean it."

"...Okay."

Nakajima began sobbing quietly.

All of a sudden I felt like I was with a little boy, and my heart ached. Because he cried like a child. It was as if his tears had nowhere to go, they were meant for god alone. I wanted to hug him to me, but I thought that might frighten him, too. So I tried something else.

"Here," I said, "let's hold hands as we sleep."

I took his hand in mine. He had been hiding his eyes with

the other hand since he started crying. And now he was crying even harder. I kept squeezing his thin, dry hand.

The heat in his palm made me think that sometimes it's too late, some things can't be fixed. I didn't know anything about his past, but I had the sense that long ago, someone had abused him sexually. He had been completely crushed, pushed to a point where there was no hope he would ever recover—or maybe it was just a matter of giving it time, I thought.

I felt bad for having spoken so flippantly. It's so easy to be insensitive about things you have no personal experience of. I couldn't even guess what it was that had gone wrong inside him.

No doubt every little thing I did to try and help him feel better, things any woman would do, only drove him further into a corner.

At the same time, seeing how extremely sweaty his face had become when he made his confession earlier had left me feeling a little frightened myself, like he was telling me more than I needed to know. Right now I was still too exhausted, too wasted to start anything new, but after a little while I hoped I could fall in love, and have more fun, and be young. Go to the movies, argue, meet up somewhere, go out to eat (even though Nakajima didn't like eating out), do all that, wasting time in a nice way. That's what I wanted to do. I didn't want to deal with weighty matters. That's what I was hoping for, except that if I were to go out with him it seemed unlikely we could ever go to a hot springs together, and simply having sex would be an ordeal. That would really be a pain. I mean, I want to have fun with my life, I thought. Because I was still able, at that point, to treat it all lightly.

And then, peering at me with the eyes of a boy in elementary school, his voice stuffy from crying, Nakajima spoke.

"Is it all right if we try? If we see if I can do it? If I can't now, I feel like I never will."

Okay, if you want, I said. And that was it.

He said he'd be too scared if we were naked, so we fumbled over each other's bodies in our pajamas. Nakajima was kind of oddly built, and he didn't really seem to be enjoying himself. It felt like I was faking sex with a person who thought sex was a bad thing.

The whole time, I kept thinking that it would take a pretty major shift in perspective for me to start wanting to go on doing this with this guy, and that made it even more bizarre.

But occasionally something in our movements flashed. There was hope.

Those are my memories of our first night together.

After I said goodbye to my mom, my life seemed to turn rapidly in a new direction.

I no longer had to go back to my hometown all the time and Nakajima had begun coming over, and everything happened so suddenly ... day after day, it was like living out some weird fantasy. Like I was inhabiting someone else's dream, some stranger's. *Did all that really happen?* I wondered, dazed, casting my mind back. To her bones, the crematorium.

And then I got offered a big job.

I was a fledgling painter, you see, who specialized in murals.

My palette was unusual, unlike other painters', so every so often my work got featured on TV programs and stuff, and since I was happy to go anywhere, all on my own—except that I often had to hire a student to take me, since I don't drive—I had gotten a decent number of jobs, here and there. It's not like I was famous or anything, but there's always a demand for that kind of work, more than you'd expect, and so I was constantly going off to do a mural on the side of someone's house or in a garden, on a crumbling wall outside an aquarium, on the side of a shed owned by a neighborhood association. The main point, as far as I was concerned, was to put my pictures outside, so as a rule I didn't agree to requests regarding the subject matter. I would talk things over with people, and to some extent I'd take general suggestions, like if someone said they wanted fruit, or animals, or the ocean or something. So far I had painted about twenty pictures on walls, warehouses, and playground equipment.

That said, I wasn't passionately committed to earning a

living this way or anything. I tried it once and people liked it, so I kept doing it. That's all there was to it.

Basically, I just liked the lifestyle I had when I was painting my murals. I didn't think my work necessarily had much value as art.

Sooner or later they were bound to be destroyed or painted over for bureaucratic reasons, after all, so there was no point obsessing over details. All I wanted was to have fun painting, to chat and make friends with people who came by while I worked, and for my mural to add just a little bit of warmth to the lives of the people in the vicinity.

The wall I'd been asked to paint this time was on the grounds of my old art school. It was a fairly low wall that divided the campus from a place that used to be a preschool and was now a privately run Infant Development Center. There was already a mural on the art-school side, one from a long time ago, but the side facing the center was just plain yellow. The people who hired me said I could paint whatever I wanted there.

I had nice memories of the building itself, since it was near my school and I had seen it all the time when I was taking classes, so I accepted the job immediately when an old classmate of mine, Sayuri, offered it to me. She was the center's piano teacher.

The building that housed the center was a bit old but really charming: it had been designed by an architect who grew up in the neighborhood, and he had worked hard to make it special so that future generations of children could go to school in a fresh, innovative structure.

Even when I was a student, I'd loved the center, I loved it more the more I saw it—the shape of the walls; the contour of the building itself; the yard, specially landscaped for children, with a little manmade hill—and I used to have my lunch leaning against that wall, watching the kids. The building had such an aura of warmth to it that I thought if I had been young enough, I would have wanted to go to school there myself.

Apparently it was getting dangerously run-down, though, and since it would cost a fortune to fix it up, someone had suggested that the whole structure be torn down. A TV crew came to report on it and everything. They presented it as the story of a community trying to save a local building and a painter they had hired to help. I agreed to do an interview.

I wasn't particularly involved with the political stuff, though. I just wanted to have fun with the kids who had to pass by to get in and out of the building, and to look into their eyes, and put the things I saw in them up on that wall. I figured this job would keep me busy all spring; beyond that, I couldn't say. There's no point thinking about the future.

That's what it's like when you're creating things. On the one hand, it really seems like you're keeping it all moving on your own, and you can tell yourself that you've got inspiration raining down on you, but ultimately you can't make anything happen on your own.

I knew the kids would make it work. They would help me put something eternal onto that wall. Something that would last forever, even if the wall did end up being knocked down. And that was enough for me.

I'd been through so many unfamiliar things recently, looking after my mom and managing her funeral and so on, and it was like this worldly grime had rubbed off on me from dealing with all that. I wanted to wash it all away, throwing myself into my work.

Caring for my mom had taken all the energy I had, and I hadn't had the mental space to think of anything but how overwhelmed I was. I'd always felt that I was striving for something good, though, reaching toward the light, and so it really hadn't been that bad. Things had come to feel so normal that I could hardly believe it when I would remember I couldn't call her up to talk whenever I wanted to anymore, about whatever was on my mind.

I had always been thinking about her, about what I could do for her, but she would be unconscious, or in a daze, out of it. That was what really hurt.

The meeting that afternoon went smoothly.

I had a pleasant discussion with the managers of the Infant Development Center—a couple who had worked, apparently, in a preschool in the United States—and we agreed that I would paint a cheery group of animals or something along those lines. I was a bit troubled by the bumpiness of the wall, but it would take too long and be too expensive to fill in all the depressions, and I had the feeling I could obviate the need by brushing on a heavy undercoat. There was nothing but dirt in front of the wall, so I wouldn't even have to spread a plastic sheet.

These things would make the work a lot easier, and it sounded as if the local government could help out financially; I'd have about five hundred thousand yen, which was enough to allow me to hire a driver for at least a few days. Having a helper would make things much easier: it was a boon to have a car, of course, and he could help me lug the twenty or so cans of water-based paint I'd need back and forth every day. I got permission to borrow the school's ladder, and with a bit of luck it sounded as if I might be able to leave my tools in the storage room, as long as there was space. Everything was getting off to a good start. When you're working at a semi-public site like this, the least bit of friction at the beginning can make things drag on and on. It looked as though things were going to work out this time.

I wonder if Nakajima will come stay over tonight, too? I thought as I stood gazing down the length of the wall, all alone.

I wasn't exactly excited, but I felt a warm glow inside.

I felt like someone with a brand-new boyfriend.

Sometimes, though, I imagined what it might be like if I happened to fall passionately in love with someone else, and it became inconvenient to have Nakajima around. What would I do then? At the moment, I wasn't really sure. He'd had a tremendous influence on me, that was true, but that seemed kind of different from being head over heels in love.

Right now it wasn't really an issue, because I was enjoying myself, but it would be a pain if something like that happened after we had become more deeply involved.

And what would happen to Nakajima if I *did* meet someone else and just chased him out? How did I know he wouldn't kill himself, or go crazy?

I couldn't begin to imagine how someone like him, with his awful past, might feel because I had never suffered any terrible wounds. Of course, it would be even worse if I thought I could understand. Recognizing how totally ignorant you are is the only honest way to deal with people who've been through something traumatic.

Still, I had the feeling it would be okay. I would go on liking Nakajima.

I had taken such great care to reach this point, and now, little by little, I was falling in love. Even putting it in conservative terms, it would probably be fair to say that I *needed* him—no one else would do. I had the sense that he was the one.

It's like when you decide to build a house: some people want to go and find the land first, then hire an architect to help them draw up the plans, and then choose the materials for the walls and everything all on their own. I'm not like that. I prefer to wander around until I stumble across something, then do the best I can with it, scrutinizing this thing I've discovered, getting to know it for what it is.

By the same token, some muralists will neatly fill in all the joints in a wall, transform it into a perfectly white canvas, come up with a motif that harmonizes with the colors around the wall, then carefully block out the sketch on their pad and enlarge it. That's one method.

But I'm not that type at all. I just lose myself in the joy of painting, getting the picture up there, and if something goes wrong in the creative process I find a way to fix it and finish the project, no matter what. I'm a real believer in working on site, and I'll be there no matter what's going on in my life, and I don't put any stock in whatever it is that happens inside my head. I look, I sense time passing, I move my body, and I try as much as possible to stay outside.

And usually, when it's all over, I find that everything has come together surprisingly well. When that happens, I feel like I've been dancing, perfectly in time, with the world.

That sense of having partnered with the environment, the land, of moving, entranced ... and then I say goodbye to it all forever, and head for the next location.

Sure, I knew perfectly well that my way was sloppy. But for me, at that point, painting murals was more like a hobby than anything else; it wasn't a true profession. So I was content with what I did. At some point I would have to decide whether or not to make this my occupation, and I assumed that as time passed, the problems that arose because I did things this way would sort themselves out in a manner that was right for me. And who knew, maybe in the process I'd become a professional painter. I figured that if I could refine my method as much as possible, and if things went as well as I hoped, I was bound to produce good results. So I just kept pushing quietly ahead. That's the stage I was at then. I was still at the very beginning.

Of course, some people criticized me for doing things the way I did. Look at her, they'd say, painting those childish pictures, she has practically no technique, and then she has the nerve to do interviews as if she were some kind of famous artist! Stuff like that. But there was one area, just one, where I had honed my abilities to perfection, and I held to that absolutely.

Since I was painting my pictures outside, I would think and think, extremely hard, until I was sure that even decades later my work wouldn't look out of date.

If I focus very hard, right at the beginning, on the scenery and the spirit that runs through the place, I start to get an image of colors and the motif that are right for it. As long as I don't misread that, as long as I manage to put myself in complete harmony with my surroundings, and as long as I don't lose my concentration, the picture I paint will last ten years, twenty years, maybe even a hundred without looking dated. That's the one ability I have faith in.

Just as the head carpenter takes pride in the house he's built, I had made up my own mind, consciously, that I was right about this. That was settled, and I stuck to my guns. I was never wishy-washy about that. I stood up to the world, and I made my little mark. Sort of like a dog, I guess, pissing someplace to show it had been there.

I don't know if it's appropriate to treat these things like they're part and parcel of being in love, but Nakajima and I never talked about preparations or plans, even dreams. We just kept going on as we were, here and now. The two of us, on location.

I couldn't do anything. Because I could tell—I felt it.

No one else is like Nakajima. No one in the world is as peculiar as he is.

I'd never seen anyone who looked the way he did standing

by the window at night, so thin and detached. He didn't have the slightest faith in this human society of ours; he stood on the outside looking in. There was something sad in his posture, and something strong, and I wanted to go on watching him forever.

Looking back now, I can see that the way I sat gazing at his silhouette against the window in those days, I might as well have been a girl in junior high with a crush on some boy. I wanted so badly to hold his image in my mind's eye. How can he look so beautiful just standing there, I wondered. And that's really all it was.

It hits so hard...

I was staring up through leafless branches. They were spread out like a hand, and that special, weak light particular to the time when winter ends and spring gets under way was filtering down through them.

I used to come to this school every day, so I knew this place through and through. I didn't need to worry that I'd paint something weird. But still, just in case, I kept standing there. I'll make the picture a little bit sad, and a little happy, I thought. Already, like a lovely shadow, a hazy image began to project itself upon the wall.

"Heading home, Chihiro?"

It was Sayuri, the woman who had gotten me the job. I assumed she had just finished one of her piano lessons. She must be taking a break, I supposed, before the next stream of kids comes in the evening.

I love feeling the rhythm of other people's lives. It's like traveling.

"Not necessarily," I said. "You want to go to a café?"

"I don't think I have time for that," Sayuri said.

So I gave her one of the two cans of coffee I'd bought earlier.

"Still thinking about that guy?" Sayuri continued. "The weirdo. The thin one. Smart, going to college."

"Yeah, that's right. I told you a little about him, I guess? Nakajima. I'm not just thinking about him anymore, actually—I think we're dating, kind of."

"What did you say he studies?"

"He said something about research on chromosomes, but I have to confess I have no idea what that means in terms of what he actually does. Right now he's working on an article about Down's syndrome and the presence of chromosome 21 and what happens when you ... I forget, he tried to explain it to me a couple times, but it was too complex, I didn't get it at all. Hardly a surprise, I suppose, seeing as he's writing the article in English. I couldn't sneak a peek even if I wanted to."

"So it's too complicated for even you to remember. The main point is that you have no idea what the main point is—that much I get. You seem to be getting along all right, though, even if you can't make heads or tails of something that must matter a lot to him."

"It's true, I know. If only he were into cultural anthropology or folklore studies or French literature or something, it would be so much easier...."

"Then you'd be able to understand it, at least a little."

"Of course, sometimes it's better not to understand. I kind of like how our days are now. I feel more at peace than I ever have," I said. "Everything's so calm, and quiet, and yet at the same time there's something powerful—it's like living underwater. The rest of the world keeps seeming more and more remote. It's kind of like, I don't know, I don't imagine things will get any more exciting than they are now, but I can't imagine us breaking up, either."

"You just started dating and already you feel that way?" Sayuri laughed.

"I haven't asked him about it," I said next, "but it's pretty clear that something happened to him, ages ago, something really bad. But you know how it is when you're with someone, you kind of figure stuff out, right? So I decided there's no hurry, I'm not going to rush him, and I guess now things have kind of settled into place. Do you think I should ask him?"

"I don't see the need. I mean, if things are going well. I just hope that whatever that awful thing is, it isn't something *really* awful. Like he committed a crime, or ran away from his debts, or went bankrupt. Or maybe that would be okay, as long as it doesn't become an issue now."

"Yeah, well, judging from his personality I'd say it probably isn't anything like that. Who knows, maybe it'll turn out not to be such a big deal. He did tell me that he was really close to his mother, and it was a huge shock when she died. But I get the sense he's been hurt in some way much deeper than that."

"I hope whatever it is isn't still an issue."

"Oh, I think it is—I feel it. I'm just hoping it's not so bad that he can't go on living with it. And hey, he's made it this far, right? Maybe everything will be fine, and it's just a matter of going on with his life, treating it as gently as possible."

I spoke like I was praying. *Please*, I thought, *keep living*.

Nothing I could ever do would relieve Nakajima of his pain. That had only become clear once we started living together. I had seen him wake up screaming in the middle of the night and bolt up, trembling; I'd seen him break into a sweat when he found himself in a crowd; I'd seen certain kinds of music give him terrible headaches; and I'd had to listen to him telling me that for a long time after his mother died, what he wanted more than anything was to follow her. These were just fragments, but the longer we were a couple, the more I saw.

When there's a plus, there's always a minus. If there's a powerful light, the darkness that is its opposite will be just as strong. To me, Nakajima seemed like a creature in a legend, unable to control the forces raging within him.

"In this line of work, I come into contact with kids who have all sorts of troubles," Sayuri said. "Some are just cruel by nature, and some have mental problems, but other than that I get the sense that usually it's the parents who are the problem. When something happens with the parent of a really young child, something seems to get paralyzed inside, or broken, and even if it's a really tiny part, it has to be built up again. I see that pretty often. It's really true, there's something huge in people like that that can't be whitewashed over. It's like, you're at a loss for what to do, because they've been broken in so many different ways, so subtly. I'm just a piano teacher so I don't actually have to deal with that stuff, but if you're a preschool teacher or something, you have to interact with the parents a lot more, and I just think that would be so hard. There are so many messed-up families these days, too many. Screwed-up parents."

I nodded. Even out by the wall, where I was painting the mural, I could tell. There were parents and children of a sort you never would have seen before, mixed in among all the rest. I didn't think Nakajima was one of them, though. His problem was different.

"I know something happened to him, that much is clear, and it obviously wasn't a subtle sort of thing. There must have been some really big event in his past. Only in his case—well, from what I can tell, his parents were divorced, but I don't have the sense it was particularly acrimonious, you know, and I know his mother loved him really deeply, and it doesn't seem like anything happened with her, so I don't think it was a problem with his parents. That's the impression I get, judging from the bits and pieces I've heard. Above all, Nakajima himself is just such a nice person.... I know I keep repeating myself, but really the only thing I can be sure of is that something appalling happened."

"Appalling? Like how?"

"Like he was kidnapped, or sexually abused, though not by his parents."

The moment I heard myself saying that, something clicked.

Every so often, that happens. I say it, and I realize it's true. Something close to an answer lay in the words I'd just spoken. I was convinced of it. But I decided just to keep talking.

"Anyway, he's not like other people at all, it's like, I don't know how to describe it, like he's living in the clouds, maybe. Like when people talk about someone having transcended it all—he's like that, I guess. So part of me thinks it's just in his makeup, and he would have been this way even if nothing had happened. For the time being I'll just keep watching, I won't rush it. He and I are the kind of people who need to take things slow anyway. Getting to know each other, talking things through, everything has to go nice and slow," I said.

At some point, as I was talking, it hit me how deeply concerned about Nakajima I was. That I wanted to know, sort of, except that at the same time I didn't.

That was why I felt this way. As if maybe, maybe, I was starting to commit.

Maybe I'd begun to love him, maybe at some point I'd actually fallen for him in a big way. For the first time in my life I seemed to be in love, not just playing—a woman loving a man.

I could tell because I was cautious, the way my mom had been with my dad.

That's how she was: the deeper she loved, the more hesitant she was.

"How about money? Does he have his own?"

"Yes. He says his father will keep supporting him until he finishes his Ph.D., and I guess he has whatever his mother left, too. He still has his own apartment, but since he spends nights at my place he puts money in my account for food and utilities and stuff. Every month. And he calculates it all incredibly precisely. Down to the hour, down to the yen."

"He's good about those things, then."

"You're pretty down-to-earth yourself, huh, asking about that?"

"Well, anyway, it sounds to me like everything's fine. You can go on living together like you are for the rest of your lives. It's kind of weird, but then so are you."

"Yeah, I guess I'll just let things progress this way for a while," I said. Thinking to myself, *Assuming there's any progress.* "But enough about that. You came out because you had something to talk about, right?"

"Right. I wanted to apologize. For making you go on TV, about the mural."

"Oh, don't worry about it. I don't mind."

"You're really famous now, huh?" Sayuri said. "Features on TV and everything."

I laughed. "I'm certainly not *really* famous."

"In this part of town, that's enough to make you a celebrity. And a lot of people are hoping that now that you're painting this mural, if your work attracts attention, maybe the building won't be torn down after all."

"Hmm."

"I'm sorry. I didn't mean to get you involved."

"Which side are you on?"

"Oh, I don't want them to tear it down—of course not!" Sayuri said. "I live for this center. Lots of my students have been coming here for years. That's not why I suggested you, though. I just wanted to have one of your pictures here, a huge one, where I work. That's the truth. I had no intention of using you, or of making you create something only to have it destroyed."

I knew Sayuri meant it. That's the kind of person she is.

She was staring at the ground. I gazed at the fine hairs

around her ears, her thick eyebrows, and I could feel how serious she was. No doubt all kinds of people had been pressing her to do all kinds of things, but she kept it all to herself, protecting me.

"Really, I'm happy to do any number of interviews about the mural. Only, when it comes to these other things, I don't really understand the issues," I said. "Sorry."

"Thanks for being so willing to help. And on the off chance that this place should happen to be torn down sometime soon, and this wall goes with it, I'm really sorry," Sayuri said. "I'll do everything I can to protect it, as long as I'm here."

"It's okay," I said. "I don't paint for the future. Besides, it's not your fault."

"Either way, I'm planning to take a lot of pictures," Sayuri said. "And I'll have them keep copies in the district document center. That's something I'm definitely going to do."

I would have been lying if I'd said I didn't care at all whether the mural survived. But it'd be an even bigger lie to say I wanted it to survive forever. I just liked coming here and feeling things each day, and recording those feelings in a kind of big way in a picture. That was how I saw what I was doing. I guess my attitude was sort of casual.

When I compared myself to Sayuri, who was so incredibly dedicated and so earnest in her dealings with the kids, I felt sort of bad.

The truth was, it didn't make any difference to me whether

my mural was knocked down or admired or whatever. And if the Infant Development Center closed, as long as the people there were good and smart, I felt sure they would carry on their work somewhere else.

Maybe I was afraid of seeing anything as absolute. I wanted to keep moving, like a stream, and I wanted to go on watching everything from a distance.

That's how I was. I felt close to people, but I didn't have any friends I could really share my life with, our hearts melting together. Something always failed to communicate.

Nakajima was the first true friend I'd ever had, in my whole life ... I really believed that. He was extremely frail, and yet there was something in him I could trust.

I saw myself reflected in our relationship, as if in a mirror. And I knew that I wasn't wrong. And I was at peace.

All along, just because I lived away from my mom, I thought I'd achieved independence, but now that she was gone I finally realized how much, in my heart, I had depended on her.

I never asked my mom for advice, but whenever I was going through an unsettled period like I was now, I'd call her up to talk, or go back to visit, just to see her face. Now that she was gone, I realized these little things had given me a core to hold on to—or maybe brought me back, for better or worse, to the place I came from. I wasn't even sure what that meant ... whether that place was something that had existed before I was born, or not.

When I was young, I used to turn and look back at my mother's face to make sure I knew where I was in relation to her; now, I had to take stock of my situation by myself. Sure, I could see myself through Nakajima, but the second I glanced away I lost it. Parents are absolute; he wasn't.

I'd watched my mother dying for so long that now I could hardly remember how, back when she was healthy, her spirit used to shine. All that came to me now was the agonizing sound of her final breaths, the smell of her dying body that had filled the hospital room, things like that. The sense of powerlessness, knowing that my mom was suffering alone, and that in her universe I was no help at all—I could recapture that feeling, but nothing else.

I read in some book that if you try to hold people back too much when they're dying it keeps them from being reborn as a Buddha, and that had stuck with me, somehow, maybe more than it should have, so I tried hard not to cry too much, and kept telling my mom how much I appreciated all she had done for me. Now all I can do is think how stupid I was to act like that. I should have cried my eyes out. I should have thrown myself wailing at the coffin the way my dad did, and made a huge commotion. Forgotten everyone watching, the mourners and what they'd think, and just been myself.

If I had done that, I bet my mom wouldn't have come in my dream the way she did that night, worried because she saw that part of me was holding back, unwilling to fall completely in love with Nakajima.

About two weeks after Nakajima first stayed over, he asked me for a favor.

"I want to go see some old friends, but I'm scared to go alone. Will you come?"

We hadn't had sex again since that first time, but he'd been staying over at my apartment every night. He always made sure to remind me that he'd recalculate the utility bills.

My mural-painting days wouldn't start until the following week, so the timing was perfect.

Since I had so much time on my hands, I'd been cooking all kinds of dishes using a huge package of imported gourmet ham that my dad had sent. Fried rice with pineapple and ham, ham and steak, steamed rice with ham, and so on.

I tried so many different ham recipes that finally even Nakajima, who really wasn't particular about what he ate and generally was fine with anything, blurted out, "Can we have something besides ham tonight?"

Other than that, all I did was go with the guy I'd hired to help me work on the mural—a guy I knew from art school, younger than me—to buy the paints and assemble the various brushes I'd need, and then I sat at my desk working on preliminary sketches. It was a pleasant time.

I love sitting at my desk drawing—it's like painting in miniature. Since I never simply transfer my sketches to a wall, it's all about getting a sense of the partially formed image I have in mind—I'm just doodling, basically. But drawing on a small scale has its own particular pleasures. It's like when I used to play house as a kid. Tiny little utensils, tiny little people. And yet everything is blown up to actual size in my mind. That's the kind of pleasure I get out of drawing.

The wall I'd be painting was long and low, so I planned to do something bold with a lot of monkeys linked in a kind of flow, but I was having a hard time envisioning a design for it, something that would look good and fit well with the site. I couldn't believe how poorly my imagination was serving me, and I started wondering if maybe it would be best to just go and start painting, or maybe take a survey of the kids. I was coming to the end of my rope.

If I were just going to paint the sort of design an amateur could come up with, they might as well call in a bureaucrat from city hall to do the job. There needed to be a touch of eeriness in it, something private. But what? What sort of memories involving monkeys did I have—when, come to think of it, was the last time I had even seen a monkey? Should I go to the zoo to see some? Those are the kinds of issues I was grappling with. So when Nakajima asked if I would accompany him, it sounded like a great way to get my mind out of its rut.

"Sure," I said, eyeing a magazine. "Maybe we can have a picnic on the way!"

But when I glanced up and saw the expression on Nakajima's face, the lighthearted feeling with which I'd replied withered. I could see this was important to him.

Until then, things had been going along the same as always, without any trace of progress. We had gotten up that morning, shared an omelet that I'd made with our last eggs (and ham, needless to say); just then, I was sitting in a rather shocking pose, in the middle of doing my toenails, and Nakajima was tapping away on his PowerBook, working on a report. I'd just been thinking that when he got to a stopping place maybe I'd make some tea when he mentioned his friends and wanting to go see them.

Sayuri had been right: Nakajima wasn't like us. She and I had gone to an art school that wasn't very prestigious; he went to a university one district over that only people who are really, really good in school can get into.

Naturally, I asked him about it. "How did you get so good at studying? Did you like studying from the time you were little? Was that it?"

Nakajima sat thinking for a while without moving. Then he said, "One day, all of a sudden, I felt this powerful urge to study, as if I were trying to get something back that I'd lost."

"Was that ... after your mom died?" I asked.

"Yes. You see, during the time when I was away, my mother and father started arguing about all kinds of things, and then they started living apart, and in the end they divorced. Since then I've been in a situation sort of similar to the one you're in now—I still get living expenses and tuition and stuff, and I still go visit my father from time to time, and ... well, anyway, the point is that I was in high school when my mother died, and I decided I didn't want to go live with my dad. I mean, he'd been living up in Gunma since the divorce—that's the prefecture he grew up in—and I didn't really feel like moving to a new place, just like that. He had remarried, too, and they had kids. So I decided I'd live on my own, and then, well, I had enough money so it wasn't like I had to work like mad to make ends meet or anything, and I'm certainly not a big spender, so all of a sudden I found myself with lots of time on my hands. I thought a lot about what I should do. I wanted something where I wouldn't have to deal with people too much, and where I could keep my involvement to a minimum, so I'd be able to do my own stuff, and ideally I thought it'd be nice if I could make people's lives better—that's the life I wanted. And after looking into various options, I settled on genetic research."

"But why would you want to pick something so difficult?"
I said. "Did you know someone around you who did the
same kind of thing?"

He paused awkwardly again before he continued. "Well,
yeah. When I was away from my parents, the one adult I felt
close to had graduated from a department like that with a degree in genetics, and hearing about the topic from him made
me think it might be interesting to learn more. And then
after my mother died, I was all alone and I was depressed,
and since I had nothing else to do I studied constantly. I was
totally obsessed. Of course, it was all focused on passing the
entrance exams for university. I didn't want to deal with people, so I didn't go to cram school or anything, I just did it all
myself."

He went on to explain his methods in detail, at great
length.

I wanted to ask why he'd been separated from his parents,
but I didn't. I just listened.

He said he taught himself to concentrate really fiercely,
to cut his mind off from his body. He found that it wasn't all
that hard, but he also discovered that it was a dangerous thing
to do in the real world.

The story was as strange as his tone was bland.

By the time he got into the university he was aiming for, he
weighed forty-five pounds less than he had before he started.
He had stopped being able to eat at all, and he collapsed on

a road somewhere and found himself in the hospital. They had to feed him through an intravenous drip—otherwise he wouldn't have survived.

"Sounds like the wrong way to go about becoming a doctor," I said.

He laughed like crazy at that. It's true he's in the graduate school of medicine at his university, but he said none of the students in his program are training to become doctors. It's a program for future researchers.

Once Nakajima started studying he couldn't stop, and his grades got even better when he figured out how to detach his mind from his body; he got so engrossed in what he was doing that he felt as if he could have forgotten about his body altogether.

"The only thing was," he said, "I realized then, in a pretty painful way, that there's always a lag before the body responds to the orders the mind sends out."

"A lag? What do you mean?"

"It was fairly easy in the beginning, when I'd do this self-hypnosis thing, setting it up so that my body would function at the absolute minimum and all the energy would get routed to my mind instead. That much was no problem, and I guess that made me overconfident. The catch was—I'm not sure how to explain it, but it's like the process accelerated once it got underway, and even if I sent out the order to my body to engage again so that I could get some nutrition and move my limbs and stuff, even when I was really trying, it was like a merry-go-round, the way it can only stop very gradually, by spinning slower and slower. I hadn't taken that into account, and I had ignored my body too long, and so I stopped the merry-go-round too late. I almost died."

"All right," I said, "I realize that you *can* do that. But don't, not anymore, okay? It puts too much of a strain on your body. You end up paying for it later on, right?"

"That's why I don't study like that anymore. I do just enough to keep up."

Nakajima smiled.

Wow, I thought. This guy says he's doing just enough to keep up, and he can still succeed in grad school, not to mention that whenever he's not studying he's writing another article or doing some sort of preliminary research, surveying the literature or something.... He must be really good at this academic stuff. I was impressed.

"I studied my ass off all that time, and then one day, just like that, it hit me. I'm on track to finish my coursework, there's no question about that, and as long as I keep at it with the articles I'll definitely get my Ph.D. And then I can go on the market in Japan, and the chances are that there will be a good match somewhere, and I'll find a position at some institute. Only I'm not sure that the future will be all that bright if I just go on like this—if I stay here in Japan, I mean. So I've been mulling things over. I kind of think it might be good to go somewhere else. That never occurred to me before. Until now, it was all I could do just to stay alive."

All along, Nakajima's tone had remained measured and easy.

"That's not anything I'd know about," I said, "but if you've been able to manage this much, I'm sure you can do anything. I mean it—anything. You just have to put your mind to it."

Somewhere else. I.e., somewhere outside Japan. I.e.... we split up?

So as far as he's concerned, my apartment is just one step in the great escape?

I had the feeling that it wasn't yet time to talk about that.

Nakajima had said he wanted to go see his friends, and yet whenever he talked about it his expression got incredibly gloomy. So I asked him about it.

"Do you feel a *need* to see these friends of yours now?"

"No, it's not that," he said. "I feel like maybe now I *can*."

"If I come along, you mean?" I asked.

"Exactly ... I mean, you're so cheerful," Nakajima said.

"Maybe I'm not as cheerful as you think," I replied.

It wasn't that I was annoyed; I just didn't want to let him down.

I had the feeling that Nakajima was taking one aspect of

me—the straightforward, easy-going part that emerged when I was with him, the cheerful surface that I had inherited from my mom—and blowing it all out of proportion. If so, he might feel terribly betrayed when my dark, somber side eventually showed its face.

"No, I know that, it's just ... I know I can't express it very well, no matter how I phrase it, but *you're just right*. This sounds kind of odd, but your proportions are just right."

I sort of knew what he was trying to say.

Considering how smart Nakajima was, I bet he could have found a way to express more precisely what it was like to push his body to the limit while studying, or his perspective on the way my emotions were structured inside me. He was just being nice, communicating on my level. That's what made it sound vague.

Still, I had the sense that right then it helped for him to be talking about something, and so I decided to draw him out. I intentionally cocked my head slightly, feigning puzzlement.

"I mean, for you love is more important than anything else, right, Chihiro?" Nakajima said. "But you don't try to control other people, do you?"

"I guess that's pretty true," I replied.

"And you cherish the memory of your mother? Of course, everyone has little knots in their hearts, no matter what their families are like—but wouldn't you say that in your case you

73

feel love and hate in ordinary, healthy amounts? Even if one may seem a bit stronger at times?"

"Yeah, I'd agree with that."

"And you don't hate your father, do you?"

"No, I don't. If anything I think he's kind of lovable. The environment we lived in wasn't ideal, but I suspect that it actually made it easier for us to express our love than in your average family. We didn't fit into any ready category, so we all had to work that much harder."

"Exactly—you don't have that sense that you can take your family for granted, that's why I feel so comfortable with you. You see your family members for what they are, and you look at me in an ordinary way, without wishing that I was some-how different," Nakajima said, his tone very level. "That's what I like about you. I'm extremely, almost pathologically sensitive to violence, and I pick up on it immediately when something violent is happening. Most people are constantly perpetrating little acts of violence on others, even when they don't mean to. You almost never do that, Chihiro."

"How about you?" I asked.

"I've never been able to discuss this before," Nakajima said, "but honestly, I felt oppressed the whole time until my mother died, because of the way she was always fretting over me—no one else mattered. She became so focused on me that ulti-mately my father got fed up and left. It really weighed down on me, but at the same time certain things had happened

to keep us apart for a long time, and during that whole period I'd yearned to see her so badly. But then when we were
finally reunited, when she was actually there, in person, her
love completely overwhelmed me.... Like, if I was going out
for a while, she couldn't rest easy unless she'd checked to see
when I'd be coming home, and if I was even a minute late
she would be waiting up, crying, you know? That's the kind
of woman she was.

"And to make matters even worse, she died before we'd
had time to live together as long as most mothers and sons do,
and so I felt even more confused. I have these two different
images of her etched into my memory: one as this idealized
mother, and the other as a sort of pressure weighing down on
me—obsessive, feminine love.

"The ideal side of her, though—that part of her was so
extraordinary, it just blew me away, and I felt so small beside
her, and I know that if it hadn't been for her I wouldn't even
be here today. I'm so grateful to her that if she were still alive,
I could spend my whole life trying to pay her back and it
would never be enough.

"There was one time in particular when things got really
terrible. There was a period when we were like a couple in
love, lost in our own maze with no way out. We were both
going regularly to the hospital then, and we were in such bad
shape that our doctor suggested we go and spend some time
in a small house that belonged to some relatives of ours. It

was a run-down shack way out in the country with nothing around it, and we did stay there for a while, living a quiet life. It was cool in the summer, but in the winter it got incredibly cold, we were always freezing, but the scenery was gorgeous, you could always see the lake, and it was lonely, and beautiful.

"And now those friends of mine, the people I've been talking about, they live there now, and I want to go see them, I've been trying, but whenever I think about it—just look at me, you can see how it makes me sweat. I've thought about going any number of times these past few years, but every time I end up making all sorts of excuses to myself, and in the end I decide not to go. No matter how hard I try, I can't for the life of me figure out what it is that makes me break out in a sweat like this—my memories of my mother, or the memories I share with my friends."

"If it brings back such painful memories, maybe you don't need to go," I said. "Why don't you just wait until it starts to feel right? Don't force it. Go when you're ready."

Nakajima looked miserable when I said this.

"If I do that, I won't ever get to see them. I'll never see my friends again."

"When's the last time you met?" I asked.

"I haven't been out since before my mother died, she and I visited together ... it's been about ten years, I guess. Maybe longer. Though occasionally I call," Nakajima said.

"You really want to see them?"

"I really do, more than anything else in the world," Nakajima said. "I want to see them so badly I can't stand it. All the
time. Lately, now that I'm with you, I've been feeling more
desperate than ever to see them, like I can't hold myself back
anymore."

"And how many friends are we talking about?" I asked.

"Two," Nakajima said. "They're brother and sister, both
old friends."

I had no idea where Nakajima wanted to take me, but
I trusted him implicitly. I trusted him with my whole body,
even with my skin. When you're with someone every day, if
there's even the tiniest glimmer of a contradiction inside them,
you pick up on it. Nakajima was an uneven sort of character,
it was true, but he always struck me as totally sincere.

"All right, then, let's go. Is it far?"

"About three hours, including changing trains."

"Will it be expensive?"

"I'll pay. I'm the one dragging you along, after all."

"That's okay. I'll enjoy the trip, too."

"No, I should get the tickets and everything."

"Really, I'm in pretty good financial shape now." I laughed.
"I've got a job."

"Why are you so willing to go with me, anyway?" Nakajima said, looking a bit surprised. "You don't even know
where it is. I'd never be able to go on a trip like that."

"It's someplace you really want to go, right, even though it hurts?" I said. "It's only natural that I come along, if I'm the only person who's able to help you do that. After all, you're here in my apartment every day. We see each other all the time, and we're together because we like being together, not because we have to be."

If I were *really* in love, I don't think I could have said that. I probably would have tried to toy with his feelings a bit more, or maybe I would have had trouble finding the words. But all I felt then was a desire to help. And while I didn't yet know the reason, it frightened me much more to think of him getting hurt than it did to think of someone else getting hurt. Just the idea made me shudder, and left me feeling as if a heavy stone had lodged in my chest.

"Thank you," Nakajima said quietly.

The next day, we took a train headed north.

We got off at a small station and started walking. There was still a chill in the air—it was the sort of weather that makes your face feel cold, but doesn't do anything more than that.

From time to time, a cool ray of sunlight shone through the clouds.

There were trees everywhere, their new leaves just beginning to appear. Even the greenest branches were dotted, here and there, with sensuous, round buds, clenched but swelling, vibrant in the haze of fresh growth. The air was clear; I could feel it coursing through my body. Soon we had left behind the kernel of activity around the small-town station, and after that it was just Nakajima and me ambling along nondescript streets. The mountains in the distance were still capped with snow. That white and the brown of the trees rolled on and on under the blue sky, a dry pairing of colors.

Then, at last, we came to a small lake.

It was a weekday, so there was no one around. The water was so still you almost felt like it would absorb any sounds that reached it. The surface might have been a mirror. Then a wind blew up and sent small waves drifting across it. The only sound was the chirping of birds that whirled around us, high and low.

"It's over near that shrine." Nakajima pointed. "Where my friends live."

A small red *torii* was visible on the far shore of the lake.

I looked up at Nakajima. He was sweating buckets, and his face was pale.

"Are you okay?"

I took his hand in mine.

"I'm okay. This is the hardest part. I'll be fine once we actually get there."

Nakajima's hand was frighteningly cold.

What horrors had he endured? I wondered. Physically, emotionally.

Poor guy. Those were the words that came to me. There wasn't anything else I could say. I knew my sympathy was useless, but I couldn't help it, I pitied him so deeply. I felt sorry for him for having had to find a way, somehow, to pull himself together, far from his parents.

An awful struggle was playing itself out inside him now. That much I could tell.

From my perspective, we were simply taking a nice walk around the edge of a lake, amid lovely scenery, on an invigorating early spring day. But Nakajima didn't see that. He was in such pain he might as well have been in hell, dragging chains behind him with every step.

"Hey, Nakajima, hold on," I said.

"Huh...?" He was in a daze, clammy with sweat.

"Sit down a second."

He was obviously dying to get this over with as quickly as possible, and he looked annoyed and reluctant, as though he wished he could knock me over and run on ahead. I could see that. I clearly sensed that he wanted to refuse. And yet, for my sake, he grudgingly squatted down.

It's only in the early days of a relationship that we have to put up with such things. Soon each person figures out what the other dislikes, and stops doing those things. So at this stage it was all right, I told myself, I could still do this.

Okay, so that was just me making excuses. Ultimately, I guess I'm one of those people who always thinks with her body.

I crouched down beside Nakajima, threw my arms around him, and squeezed. Without saying a word, for a very long time. All along, I heard his breath hitting against my neck. There was a dusty odor in his hair. The sky was incredibly far away, and beautiful enough to make a person wonder why our hearts are never so free. The wind that gusted over the lake was chilly, and carried the faintest hint of the sweetness of spring.

We stayed like that until Nakajima's breathing calmed and he stopped sweating.

There was a kind of intensity in us then, but it wasn't sensual. Neither of us was in control enough for that. I was the one hugging him, and yet I felt as if we were clinging to each other, he and I, at the edge of a cliff.

Sooner or later, he's going to disappear.

I felt sure of this. However much I loved him, and as beautiful as the world was, none of it was powerful enough to take the weight off his heart, that heaviness that dragged him down, into the beyond, making him yearn to be at peace. My body sensed it. And my soul.

But this memory will remain, I thought.

Otherwise, what point was there in his being born? Tears welled in my eyes.

"Thanks, I'm okay now," Nakajima croaked, even though he wasn't okay.

Then he gave my hand a squeeze and coldly shook me off.

When we had walked on awhile, my vision started clouding. I thought maybe I was having an anemic spell because I'd hugged Nakajima so hard before, and from worrying so much. I started having some trouble breathing, too. It was like his suffering had rubbed off on me.

"I'm sorry, whenever I try to visit them—I simply can't do it," Nakajima said, noticing what was happening. "I can't help thinking about stuff, even though I shouldn't."

"That's only natural," I said. "You're always talking about how you can't do things. I wish you wouldn't. I don't want to hear that. It makes my ears ache just listening to you."

"I know, it's a habit. It's because I used to be in an environment where you either had figured out how to do things well or you died."

"Really...?"

The people we're on our way to see hold the key to all this, I thought. And maybe when he tells me about them, he'll share something of his own past, too. There was a point in his life when that's how things were. I do want to know. When you love someone, you want to know. Even about the things that are hard for them.

The lake had started looking blurry, and I realized a mist had gathered. All of a sudden, the world before me was shrouded in it. The lake, seen through the mist, was submerged in a pale, milky white, as if a gauzy curtain hung between it and me.

We kept walking. The path faded into the haze, and we found ourselves padding along with no view of what lay ahead. He's used to walking here like this, I noticed. Even tiny lights oozed outward, acquiring round, glowing halos.

"Hey, there it is," Nakajima said.

Beyond the red *torii* was a narrow stone stairway that led up to a small shrine. From up there you would have a good view of the lake. Straining my eyes, off in the distance to one side of the *torii*, I saw a house. It was just as he had described it: a run-down shack. When I saw that wooden structure, blurred by the mist, I wondered if it even had electricity.

A few missing steps in the front stairway had been replaced with boards. Holes in the windows were covered with scraps of plastic sheet. It seemed pretty dim inside.

Looking more closely, though, I saw that the boards and the plastic had been put up with great care, very simply, in the most practical way. Everything looked old, but it wasn't dirty or unkempt. It called to mind the phrase "honest poverty."

Various little signs here and there suggested that the people inside were living proper lives: the potted plants, for instance, and the way spokes shone on the ancient bicycle that stood off in an unobtrusive corner, even though there was a hole in the basket.

"Hello!" Nakajima shouted.

The house was as still as the lake—so quiet I wondered if anyone was there after all. But after a few moments, someone wandered out.

He was an adult, perhaps thirty-five or so, and yet he was extremely small, like a child. His face seemed kind of shrunken, giving him the look of a bulldog. His eyes were sparkling, though, and there was something noble in the way he carried himself.

"Hey, it's Nobu! You really came!" the man said.

He had on a sweater covered in fuzz and a well-worn pair of khakis, but he still looked as tidy as the house. His long hair was pulled into a neat ponytail, and while he was a bit plump he stood perfectly upright. He made a very good impression on me.

"Mino! It's been ages!"

Nakajima was beaming. There was no trace now of the fear and trembling he had endured at the thought of seeing this friend.

I guess you could say he was acting like a man. You could also say he was a pain in the neck, making me worry so much when he was going to be just fine in the end. Either way, I was flabbergasted by the change.

Seeing him like this, I wondered how much he might still be hiding from me. I could see we had a long way to go.

"So at last you've come to see us," the man said. "I heard about your mother.... I'm sorry. But I guess it's been a while since that happened, too, hasn't it." He gave a little smile. A cute smile that lit up his whole face.

"I know—it took time for me to finally make myself come. I wanted to see you so badly, but it made me anxious. This place is full of memories of my mother—it gets me down. . . ." Nakajima gazed up at the roof and squinted. Then he turned to me. "It was okay, though, because I've got a guide. I finally made it."

"Nice to meet you," Mino said, looking my way. "And her name . . ."

"Chihiro. She's my girlfriend. Chihiro, this is Mino," Nakajima said.

I smiled and said hi, my mind awhirl with all I didn't understand.

There was something special in their intimacy. They could smile back and forth without speaking, like soldiers who had fought side by side.

The wind was beautiful, racing through the sky.

If only we could live someplace like that, so high and lovely, free as birds, liberated from our worries. But we don't, and I have to confess that Nakajima was a weight on my shoulders. Not a heavy one, but a weight nonetheless. Until lately, I'd lived in a world all my own, and I didn't like the idea that Nakajima might come to depend on me more than he already did. I didn't *really* dislike it, but I didn't like it. In short, I was ready to make a run for it. *I don't want this responsibility*, I thought. *I don't want to be part of the gloominess these not-normal people exude.*

Mino peered at me, grinning, as these thoughts ran through my mind.

And all at once I felt content, as if I had an angel watching over me. I didn't even feel that I had to hide what I was thinking. His eyes were so clear it seemed as though all the bad bits of my personality were being swept away, just like that.

"What about Chii?" Nakajima asked. "How's she doing?"

"She's inside. Come on in," Mino said. "Sorry it's so cramped and dirty."

Nakajima and I nodded to each other and went inside.

The inside of the house was as plain and tidy as a European country cottage, the kind you see in movies.

As far as I could tell, the first floor only had a kitchen, a toilet, and a bath. Mino led the way into the kitchen, and after we had each picked a chair we thought we could sit in from the mismatched group around the table, we gingerly sat down. The table was perfectly square, like an oversized school desk.

"I used to live here with my mother," Nakajima said. "It was like camping, like in an old French film—we didn't have much, but every day we would gather up whatever we could find, and we lived like that, very quietly. Always looking at the lake."

"Wow," I said.

"It was hard sometimes, but in retrospect I had a lot of fun." Nakajima had gotten a bit hyper, and his tone was cheerful. "The house is so small, we used to go on walks every day. Just wandering around the lake. Sometimes we'd go out in a boat, too. We felt better each day. People look so beautiful when their expressions show that they know they have a future. You couldn't help seeing how my mother was reviving—it was like watching the mountains turn green, the trees growing new leaves. I remember it so clearly, all that, how happy it made me."

Tears filled Nakajima's eyes as he spoke.

The whole house was still. Outside the window there was nothing but the lake, hazy in the early spring.

To me, it was a frighteningly desolate scene.

Mino brought water to a boil over a low flame, and carefully made tea.

I took a sip. A delicate fragrance filled my mouth. This was the most delicious black tea I had ever drunk in my life.

When I told Mino this, he fidgeted shyly.

"The springs here are good for tea," he said. "I go and get water every day, just for tea."

No way, it can't just be the water, I thought. It's because this is all he has, in this circumscribed world. Looking out at the lake, drinking good tea. That's his only luxury.

And what an enormous luxury that is. He's created a world

for himself that no one else can interfere with, I thought. A world free from all external impositions.

Mino's bearing was sufficiently dignified to expunge the last traces of a middle-aged-lady-poking-her-nose-into-everything sort of sympathy that had managed, in some mysterious way, to keep smoldering inside me, until then.

Good tea is eloquent enough, it turns out, to change a person's mind.

Nakajima and Mino exchanged various bits of gossip for a while, giddy as two schoolboys. I half listened, staring out at the lake. Sometimes there were waves, and for a second it would look very cold, and then it went back to being a mirror ... I watched the water near the shore, smooth as a piece of fine cloth, through the glass.

"Actually, I had a question I wanted to ask Chii. It's not a big deal, though, if she's in bed," Nakajima said.

"What are you talking about?" Mino replied. "She's always asleep. Let's go see her."

Then, for a long moment, he peered at me. And then he spoke.

"You see, Chii, my younger sister, has been bedridden for ages. She's not exactly sick, but her liver and kidneys aren't in good shape, so she doesn't have much energy—it's hard for her to move around. So she really is always in bed. Even when she gets up to go to the bathroom, she has to sort of slide along the wall because her muscles have atrophied. She hardly eats at all, either: only one meal a day, and basically it's just rice porridge and saké. She almost never gets up. I guess you could say she's sick, then, in a general way. But she isn't seeing any doctors, and I'm happy to give her as much attention as she needs, so we're fine just as we are, living like this. I move her arms and legs for her sometimes and encourage her to walk around the house, but I try to be as gentle with her as I can."

I wasn't sure how to respond, so I just said, "I see."

"And—well, when Chii wants to say something," he went on, "she looks into my eyes and says it inside of me, into my heart. Sometimes the information she passes on is special, and there are people who come to listen to her speak. That's how we make ends meet. Only she doesn't always have information, it's not as if she has something to say to everyone, so as a rule we try to keep all this secret. So if you don't mind, we'd appreciate it if you kept it to yourself."

"In other words ... it's like fortune-telling, in a broad sense?" I asked.

"You could think of it that way," he said. "But often it's simply a matter of enjoying the conversation. For some reason, people find that talking to her seems to bring something into focus. Perhaps it's because she spends all her time sleeping—she comes and goes just as she pleases in the world of her dreams, she's free to go anywhere she wants. And that gives her access to much more information than people have who are up all the time."

"I guess that sort of makes sense," I said. "And I won't tell anyone."

"I know. Because you had a reason to come here," Mino said. He grinned again, and the twinkle in his eyes grew even more intense, like a star. "You're welcome to come anytime you like. Only you'll never think of this place, never, unless you're meant to come."

It sounded like a riddle.

"I understand," I answered. Smiling.

He was so wonderful, a smile was all I could give him.

"Would you like to meet my sister? With Nobu?" Mino asked.

"That's okay. Nakajima deserves his privacy, and if I were her I know I'd be embarrassed meeting someone new from my bed," I said. "I'll see her next time, if I come again."

I knew how important seeing Mino and Chii was to Nakajima, and I didn't want to get in the way. My role was over now, I thought: all I'd needed to do was keep distracting him, drawing him on until he arrived. I had done my duty, and now I preferred to hang back.

"Why don't you come?" Nakajima said. "After all, she's always in bed."

"It's okay, really. You have a lot to talk about," I said.

"But I want to introduce you to Chii, too," Nakajima said.

"Who knows, maybe she'll have some information about you," Mino said mischievously.

I'm easily swayed enough that I was tempted by that, but when I thought about the past these three seemed to have shared I couldn't help feeling a bit somber, and the temptation waned.

"I'll just say hello and come right back down and wait here," I said.

"All right, then, let's go!" Mino said.

Climbing a steep, creaky staircase, we came to the second-floor landing, which was brightly lit by a small window in the hall. There were two rooms, both with their doors shut.

Mino opened one without saying a word. I tensed up, feeling a little nervous. A nice scent, like roses, wafted from the room. It wasn't roses, though—it was like a sign. A sweet sign.

"Oh, Chii! You haven't changed a bit!" Nakajima said, almost sobbing.

"Come on in," Mino said, and so I stepped inside.

There was a cheap wooden bed with a cheap pink fleece blanket on top of it, and almost buried under the blanket a small, thin woman was curled up, sleeping.

She was so tiny she could have been a child, but she was just like Mino: looking closer, I could see that she was an adult. Her body was slight, and her arms were as scrawny as bare branches; her eyelashes, long and vigorous, were the only part of her that looked different.

"Uh, she looks like she's really asleep," Nakajima said.

"No, no, she's completely awake," Mino said.

"Good, then she can hear me. Hey, Chii, it's me, Nobu—long time no see!" Nakajima said. "Sorry I didn't come visit sooner. Hey, I brought my girlfriend Chihiro along today. I wanted to introduce her to you. I've been doing really well. I went to college, and now I'm in grad school. Studying all the time."

Mino put his hands to his head. There was a pause, and then he spoke.

"Well, that's splendid. It sounds like you've been working hard!"

The voice was totally different. Okay, I thought, so this is her voice.

And what if all this is just a delusion of Mino's—what if his sister is dying of some sickness of the heart, wasting away, and Mino, unwilling to acknowledge that, is making up this internal voice of hers?

That would have been the logical response, but thoughts like that didn't stand a chance in the unique, noble atmosphere of this room.

"And, my, what a complicated woman friend you've brought along!" Mino said. "Don't you find that it ... hurts, not letting even half of your emotions out? I see you've overcome your hatred for your parents with that easygoing love you were born with. And in the process you started thinking about things, and you ended up taking on this docile personality—but aren't you really more spirited and free, more spoiled, and *extremely* into sex? At the same time, I can see you can have genuine respect for other people. You'll be coming here again before long, on your own. Let's talk more then."

I was startled when I realized she was talking to me.

The information was accurate enough, but not enough to prove this was genuine.

Mino came to his senses.

"I'm sorry," he said. "My sister tends to be a bit harsh, and she's not used to covering up the things in her heart—we used to get in trouble all the time, everywhere we went. It was so bad, sometimes I wonder if it might have been all the complaining she had to put up with whenever she opened her mouth that landed her in bed like this."

"Your sister is rather, uh, forthright, isn't she?" I said. "Only not in an unpleasant way, not really—personally, I admire that sort of bluntness."

True, her comments were pretty over the top considering that this was the first time we'd met, but I couldn't believe she was trying, for some inexplicable reason, to hurt me.

"It's kind of you to say that. And please, *please* don't think that I'm actually the one who's thinking and saying those things." Mino smiled.

I nodded goodbye and went downstairs. To tell the truth, I had absolutely zero desire to come back here and listen to her analyze my personality in even more detail. But it wasn't as though I was offended. I couldn't put my finger on the reason, but somehow I was really moved by the odd air of grace and nobility that clung to the two people who lived in this house.

I don't know what Nakajima asked Chii that day.

All I know is that it wasn't about us or how long he would live, but about a more cheerful topic. I could tell that right away from his face when he came downstairs.

And I know what he told me: "You remember the other day I mentioned that eventually, if I can finish up my degree, I want to go to Paris and work for this famous research institute? I asked her if that was possible, that's all."

Paris. He wants to go to Paris. Knowing him, he'll study like crazy and write articles and send them out like there's no tomorrow, and he'll get his degree in no time. And then I suppose this precarious life of ours will be over.

I was startled at how sad the thought made me. I could almost hear my heart breaking.

No, it's not that, I tried to tell myself, because I didn't want to admit how attached I had become to him. I'm not that heartbroken, it's just that it's so early in our relationship.

"Of course it's possible! How can you even doubt it?" I said. "I could have answered that question for you. You'll definitely be able to go."

"I have the feeling I'll find some way to sabotage myself," Nakajima said. "Though according to Chii, this time next year I might already be in Paris."

Nakajima looked truly delighted. That alone, I thought, made it worth the trip.

We had one last cup of tea and chatted a bit, and then Nakajima and I left that adorable little house behind.

Mino stood under the light outside the front door and waved to us for the longest time. His silhouette was like a lovely little shadowgraph in a locket or something, and the lightbulb beamed into the dark, shining like a jewel.

The lake had retreated into the darkness like a deep hole, turning such a deep black that only the contrast with the groves of trees indicated that there was anything there at all.

"Are you feeling pressured?" I asked. "Like you have to go to Paris right away?"

"No, I'm not rushing," Nakajima said. "I just don't really believe I can do it. I can't really explain this very well, but it's like I have this sense of guilt inside me, and sometimes it tries to mess me up. All I have to do is make myself think I can do it, just once, and then I'll be fine, because I can work toward that. Basically, I'm happy to go whenever."

"Oh, good—so you won't be going right away!" I said. "I'm so glad to hear that. Because right now I'd like to go on living like this, just as we are."

Nakajima didn't reply. I couldn't tell if he was happy or disturbed.

It occurred to me that maybe he was planning to hurl himself into his studies immediately, so he'd go back to living in his own apartment. If so, I could at least look in on him from time to time, to make sure he didn't overdo it. The thought gusted smoothly, cleanly through my mind, like a breeze sweeping across the lake's surface. As though I'd been planning something like this all along.

We were crunching our way along a gravel road now. The light from the streetlamps bled outward into circles, one white ring over the next.

Without particularly thinking about it, I had twined my arm around Nakajima's because it was dark and hard to see the road in places and I was afraid there might be snakes.

I mentioned this to Nakajima.

"No snakes yet, it's too cold," Nakajima said.

"But there might be something else. Insects, say," I said.

His arms were like sticks, but they were warm.

Suddenly he spoke. "I like this life, too. We get to go home together."

This was his response to what I'd said earlier.

I felt as though we had been walking like this forever. At the edge of this lake. Through scenery so gorgeous it seemed like another world. *I'm sure I'll walk like this with lots of other people*, I thought, *but I'll probably never feel this way again.*

Not because being with Nakajima made my heart ache, but because he made me feel how precious our time together was. It was so lovely there, and so incredibly quiet, that if even one more person had been with us I knew the mood would have been destroyed. Well, maybe it would be okay if it were someone like Mino. But it was true, I could feel it—all it would take for this delicate world of ours to come crashing down was just a single extra element. Sturdy as the bond between us was, it was also somehow terribly fragile.

"Don't go away, Nakajima," I said. "I mean, I'm not talking about Paris or anything, you can go to Paris. I just want you to do your best to stay here, in this world."

"I don't particularly want to—to go away," Nakajima said. "Only it's like there's something inside me, in my body, that's constantly telling me I don't belong here."

"You've got to fight it, Nakajima."

"I am fighting, it's just that I've lost so much, I can't fight very hard."

"Don't be a wuss," I said.

"Just look at me, though. I can hardly have sex with a girl I like."

"That doesn't matter. I'm not into sex, anyway."

"Yeah, right, you can't fool me. You're actually *extremely* into sex!"

"Now that's *rude!*" I cried.

My voice shattered the silence, and seemed to echo in the black night sky.

Nakajima was chuckling.

I sensed that he, Mino, and even Chii had something in common, though since Chii had just been lying there I didn't have much of an impression of her.

I saw it as a sort of desolate landscape, unfathomably lonely and hopeless, totally wrecked, its very foundation destroyed, but one that was being pieced together again from scraps.

Where could they have gotten to know one another? I was slowly starting to figure it out. It wasn't anything more than a guess, but I had a vague understanding, at least, of something.

It was so dark, though, I didn't even want to admit it could be part of the truth of life.

I still believed, back then, much more than I do now, that the world was essentially a happy place, full of the sounds of families having dinner together, the smile on a mother's face when she sees her husband off to work in the morning, the warmth radiating from a loved one in bed beside you when you wake up in the middle of the night.

That's not how it was with Nakajima, in his world. His universe included everything dark, and that darkness was always there. It had nothing to do, say, with him being a man and me a woman, it was a result of the different paths our lives had taken. I thought I had a pretty good grasp of the world compared to other people my age, but that was nothing compared to the weight Nakajima carried inside him.

Still chuckling, Nakajima took my hand in his, and we walked quietly on around the lake, heading for the station. It was peaceful. We decided to buy a bentō box for dinner and eat it on the train home. It felt, that night, as though each step we took brought us closer to the future.

When we turned to look back, the lake had misted over.

It seemed pale, vaguely warped.

The next week, my mural-painting days got under way.

I set out from the apartment at eight each morning, as if I were a construction worker on the way to a site. Because that's when the light is best.

I would plant a kiss on Nakajima's cheek, then head straight for my wall.

The first day, I painted a few frolicking monkeys. After

that, I decided that I would paint a big lake on the left third of the wall. Of course, I'd put monkeys around the lake, too. Calm monkeys, and lots of trees. A monkey brother and sister, and a mother monkey and her son.

I knew it would be painful to paint these things, but I couldn't stop myself.

A little girl came and said, "You're drawing monkeys?" And that got things started: little by little, children began gathering around. I seriously bawled out a few boys who were about to start messing around with my paints, and then I apologized, and after that even they slowly started to appreciate what I was doing.

One skinny little boy with big eyes and a flat nose came over and asked, "Does it mean the school won't be closed anymore when it has your picture?" Clearly Sayuri and his parents had been talking to him. People called him Yotchan, and he was taking English classes.

"No, I'm afraid not. Even with my picture, it may be closed."

"Then why are you drawing it?"

"Because there's a place to paint, and they asked me to paint it. Won't it be nicer to have some pretty colors here, even if it's only for a little while?"

"It isn't for art?"

"Hardly," I said, laughing. "Not by a long shot. It's just a picture of some monkeys."

"Um, are those monkeys ghosts?" Yotchan asked.

Following his finger with my eyes, I realized he was pointing to the four monkeys over by the lake. I had only sketched their forms, so they were just uncolored outlines, half transparent.

"No, they aren't ghosts. I'll color them in later on."

"Oh," Yotchan said. "I thought it was funny."

Children are incredible, I thought. It never would have occurred to me to paint ghosts into such a happy picture.

I kept mulling over the composition as I brushed on the colors.

The area around the lake was going to be the most colorful, and I wanted to keep it balanced with the rest of the painting, so I would probably be doing it last. But I couldn't leave those monkeys as ghosts. I'd give them some fun-looking colors, but nothing too loud, since they lived quiet lives. I'd use the happiest tones I could come up with. And I'd paint in some tea, too. And cake. I'd fill in the area around that harsh sleeping beauty with lovely, lovely colors.

Surprisingly, Nakajima didn't stop living in my apartment even after I got wrapped up in the mural and began staying out as long as the sun was up.

For some reason, somewhere in the back of my mind I'd

thought that as soon as I started working on the mural, he would vanish.

Sometimes I'd have a dream like that, and I'd wake up with my heart racing, bolting upright on my futon. Tears would be streaming down my cheeks—even I was startled. I had come home to find that Nakajima was gone, along with all his stuff. I rushed to the window, hurriedly slid it open, and looked out, but his window was dark. There was nothing to indicate that Nakajima had ever existed. To think that it was all over, so soon ... That was how the dream went.

Each time I had it, I realized again that it could happen at any time.

And yet when I came home worn out from painting, Nakajima was always there.

Sometimes he had even started the rice cooker.

Other times he was asleep, exhausted from his studies. Stacks of incomprehensible books about biochemistry and genetic engineering and so on would be stacked up next to him, their pages marked with Post-its.

Nothing about our days together was certain. The only thing I could count on was that for the time being he was still here with me, still living.

One evening, I came home to find Nakajima lying on the floor, snoring.

His PowerBook was open on the low table where we ate our meals, so I assumed he must have fallen asleep while he was working. I brought a blanket over and was putting it over him when something caught my eye.

He had something tucked under his armpit. A hard-looking silver rectangle.

It was such a bizarre sight that at first I couldn't for the life of me tell what it was. Actually, that's not quite right. Maybe I did know what it was, and my brain just refused to accept it. Because it seemed so completely out of place, so surreal.

It was an old wire rack for toasting mochi.

A chill ran down my spine. It didn't make sense.

It seemed like it would be painful to sleep with something like that stuck in your armpit, so I tried very delicately to slip it out. But he had it clamped there so tightly, like a child squeezing a thermometer much harder than necessary under his arm, that it would have been impossible to remove it without waking him.

I could see from the ferociousness with which he held on to the rack that it was extremely important to him, but even so, deep down, the discomfort I felt seeing it there lingered.

I thought long and hard about whether I should mention it when he awoke.

The thing was, I couldn't very well pretend I didn't know.

Besides, this was my apartment. Should I slip out of the room when he woke up? That seemed kind of odd, too.

I wondered what it might mean. Maybe ... that wire rack was actually the only thing that turned him on?

Did I love him so deeply that I could go along with something like that, if he had that side to him? Would I feel absolutely comfortable with it? (After all, there are all kinds of people ... I once knew a guy who could only get excited by goldfish. He couldn't masturbate or have sex or anything unless he had a goldfish in front of him.)

I wasn't sure. The honest truth was that while I *might* love him that much, it was equally likely that I hadn't yet reached that point.

I was still worrying about this when, just like that, Nakajima woke up.

He opened his eyes, bolted up in bed, and sat there dazed, unguarded, with the wire rack still under his arm.

"Want some coffee?" I asked.

"Oh, hey, Chihiro, you're back. I guess I must have fallen asleep," Nakajima said. "I didn't sleep a wink last night."

"You can keep sleeping if you want. It's all right with me," I said.

"No, I'd better get up. Coffee sounds great."

With that, he casually took the rack out from under his arm. He gave a just-woke-up sort of yawn and sat staring blankly ahead, his hair tousled.

Then at last he noticed that I was staring at the rack, look-ing like I wanted to say something, and he said, "Oh, this? It's a memento of my mother. I sleep with it under my arm when I get the feeling I'm going to have a bad dream."

"Oh ... I see," I said, surprised at how easily the mystery had been solved.

"There's no particular reason I chose the rack," Nakajima said, evidently sensing from my expression that I was won-dering what it had to do with his mom. "I just held on to it because it's something she always liked, and she took good care of it. And it's thin, so I can keep it between the pages of a book. I think it used to be my grandmother's, and we used it in our family ever since."

"That was the best memento you could find?"

"Well, I can't very well sleep with papers, and I don't wear jewelry, and stuffed animals are unsanitary, and I'd look silly wearing a woman's watch ... in the end this just felt right."

"But what made it feel right? It looks like it'd hurt."

"No, it doesn't. It's really thin."

Nakajima held out the rack, smiling.

"It's okay for me to touch it?"

"Sure."

It was just an ordinary rectangular wire rack, a little browned from use. Light and hard and cool to the touch.

As far as Nakajima was concerned, it was just another everyday tool, like a toothbrush or a razor. That kind of bewildered me. How it was weird to me, but not to him.

"You've got the hard version of Linus's blanket." I laughed.

Nakajima blushed. "So is this really unusual and embarrassing?"

It was such an adorable reaction that I couldn't suppress a smile.

"No, that's not what I meant," I said. "There's no such thing as 'unusual and embarrassing' here. We're at home, after all."

"I'm glad. I thought maybe I was doing something crazy again."

Casually but lovingly, Nakajima closed the rack between the pages of a book.

I think I must have been reeling a bit at what I had just said. Because my mom used to say almost exactly the same thing all the time about her club.

"There are no rules here, except that you have to sit properly at the bar when you drink. People can tell me anything they want. Things they wouldn't usually say, things that wouldn't be acceptable at work—it doesn't matter. That's what this place is for, after all: they come and pay money to buy themselves, their innermost hearts, a bit of freedom."

She said things like that a lot.

She'd say it whenever a customer prefaced a story with the words *I'm ashamed to admit this* or *You're going to think this is really disgraceful, but . . .*

Her openness helped set people's hearts free, including my dad's.

I guess, I thought, my mom is still alive, here inside me.

"Do you mind if I ask how you can tell you're going to have a scary dream?" I said.

"Not at all. Before I fall asleep, my eyes start moving really fast, and my head starts feeling heavy," Nakajima said, his tone perfectly ordinary. "When that happens, I know I'm definitely going to have a nightmare. I suspect it has a lot to do with how my body is doing, like if I'm particularly exhausted, or if the air pressure is particularly low—stuff like that. I can't go throw myself into my parents' arms now, of course, and I can't ask you to put up with that kind of thing, so when it happened today as I was going to sleep I just put the rack under my arm like I always do."

I nodded sympathetically, though I felt more sad than anything.

That night, watching Nakajima's back as he brushed his teeth, I cried a bit. I couldn't help crying when I thought of him sleeping with that rack tucked under his arm whenever he got lonely, ever since his mother had died, as if doing so were as natural as taking medicine for a fever, or having someone give you a scare when you can't stop hiccupping.

But what sense was there in crying?

After all, he had found a rational way to deal with his loneliness. The truth was, I thought, that I was insulting him with my tears.

And so I decided not to cry anymore.

But when I got up to go to the bathroom that night, the edge of the rack that was sticking out of the book Nakajima had put it in glinted in the dark, and that got me crying again.

Nakajima was fast asleep.

Suddenly it dawned upon me. He really isn't the sort of guy who can just go off and spend the night at someone's apartment, without giving it another thought. When he made up his mind to come here, it was because he really wanted to.

I was still pretty childish in those days—the truth is, I really *was* a child—but I prayed then, prayed until my head hurt, that I wouldn't do anything to betray his trust, and that he would go on feeling comfortable here, in my apartment, forever and ever.

I had finished outlining the mural and it was time to fill in the colors; I no longer had any uncertainties about the finished design, which I was gradually coming to see in my mind's eye. All I had to do now was keep moving toward that vision.

I enjoyed going out, spending each day moving my hands, without talking. This part was the most fun. Things progress most smoothly when the end is in view, and all you have to do is keep adding layers. I didn't have to think anymore, and things had settled down enough that I could horse around a bit with the kids. The day before, I had let some girls paint an area pink. It ended up being more trouble than I had bargained for because I had to go back and fix the places where they had gone outside the lines, but that was kind of enjoyable, too. Fortunately I wasn't really worried about keeping on a schedule.

Sometimes I found myself utterly alone. Somehow, miraculously, no one would come by, and it would be very quiet, and I was relaxed enough to notice.

So what was I thinking then, during those rare moments when I was feeling perfectly at ease, all by myself, in the absence of any children and my student helper, when even the composition of the mural had ceased to concern me? That's not something I want to share.

I lean against the wall, pour myself a cup of lukewarm coffee from my thermos.

My butt is aching, there's a crick in my neck. I feel like I'm getting a cramp in my arm. My whole body feels strangely cold.

As long as I keep moving my hands, though, I can forget all that.

That's when I notice, all at once, that I'm alone, and I discover the vast sky overhead. In the distance, the flag over the school whips madly in the wind; other than that, it's as if everything has come to a stop.

I prefer to keep the thoughts that come at times like that, as I sit drinking my coffee, to myself—the particular texture of the sadness I feel, say. I prefer to keep those thoughts private.

I've traveled a long way today, I often think to myself.

"We're having boiled tofu for dinner."

Nakajima was awake when I got home, and he welcomed me in an apron.

The scent of well-boiled *konbu* filled the room.

"You look like a gigolo," I said.

My hands and shoes were covered in all different colors of paint. I threw down my bags in a rough sort of way, like a sailor who had just come into port.

"And the lady who's keeping me is a construction worker," Nakajima said. "I can't imagine any woman coming back from the club she works at, all covered in paint and sun-tanned, with muscles like the ones you're getting."

"That's true." I laughed. "I guess I don't look much like a hostess."

I had on jeans and a sweatshirt; my hair was tied back; too much sunscreen had left my face blotchy; and I had paint all over, including on my socks and next to my nose.

"It always seems like such a waste preparing a meal for one," Nakajima said. "A waste of food and a waste of time.

But I don't feel that way at all when I'm cooking for two."

I stepped up from the apartment's entryway and peeked into the kitchen.

"Thanks for cooking," I said. "Wow, look how neatly you cut the tofu!"

The tofu in the pot was divided so precisely it looked as if he had used a ruler.

We washed our hands and sat down across from each other to eat.

My mother had always been at the club at dinnertime, and Nakajima seemed to have grown up in a rather unusual household himself, so it felt as though we were imitating some sort of lifestyle we didn't really know anything about, playing at being a happy family. Neither of us took these moments for granted, and they made us truly content. We literally ate it up.

"It's great, isn't it, just eating tofu together like this," I said.

"You know, I've been thinking," Nakajima said. "After I graduate, I've decided I'd like to get a scholarship and go to the Pasteur Institute as soon as possible. Just a little while ago I didn't think I could, but now I do—in part because Chii assured me I'd be able to do it and in part because I'm with you now, and somehow that makes me feel like I can. It looks like I'll be able to get my degree, so I've decided to go ahead and apply. Of course, I've got to ask for letters of recommendation and send in a sample article and an outline of my research and so on, and there's an exam I'll have to pass, but I looked into it and it seems they're affiliated with an institute in Japan, and there's this program now that should make it relatively easy for me to go. If I don't make it this year I can try again next year. And if I'm accepted, I'm thinking I'd like to go for at least six months."

At first it didn't even occur to me to feel lonely; I was simply glad. Nakajima could only do things he was really enthusiastic about, so it was good that he felt this way.

"What would you do, then, Chihiro?"

"What do you mean?" I said. "I'm not interested in Pasteur. All I know about him is that he did something with silkworms and invented the vaccine for rabies. And maybe that his grave is under that institute you mentioned or something? Is that right?"

"That's a pretty impressive array of useless trivia."

"I learned it all on TV. A documentary on public television."

"Ah, that explains it. It's funny, though—don't these things interest you at all, like what school I go to, and what department I'm in, and what I work on?"

"Not really. Even if you told me, I wouldn't remember. It's all DNA and human genomes and that stuff, right? And you're in med school but you aren't going to be a doctor? And you do research, I know that, but it's not like you're working on Ajinomoto or brewer's yeast or anything else I'd know about, right? Rice bran and stuff?"

"No, nothing like that, it's true. Listening to you talk, Chihiro, I really get a sense of how lopsided ordinary people's knowledge of science is."

"You think?"

"You really aren't interested, huh?"

"I do remember that you wanted to do research on blue-green algae. That's why you went into a department of agriculture, right?"

"I didn't want to study blue-green algae, I was interested in doing an experiment that used them. I'd cultivate the algae and then investigate the conditions that make it possible to inject certain genes into them. And I didn't graduate from a department of agriculture—well, I guess maybe it used to be called that, but the actual name was the Department of Biological Resources, and I was in the Biotechnology Program. It's totally different, right? And now I'm in medical school, in the Graduate School of Medicine."

"I'll never remember those things, you know—I mean, as soon as I hear blue-green algae I immediately assume it's got to be the department of agriculture, that's just the image I have. Besides, it's not like you're interested in the program I graduated from, are you?"

"The Program of Scenography, Display, and Fashion Design in the Junior College of the N. University of Arts, right? And you majored in the scenography thing, not design?"

"I can't believe you remember. Even I'd forgotten."

"I don't usually forget things like that. I only have to hear them once."

"So anyway, what was the question? What I'd do if you left?"

"I'm sure there must be tons of art schools in Paris," Nakajima said.

"Yeah, there are."

"Some half-year programs, some yearlong programs."

"I'd imagine so."

"Well, go to one! Let's go together!" Nakajima said. "I've decided I'm going to live with you like this for the rest of my life."

"What do you mean you've *decided*. Are you proposing to me?" I said, feeling suddenly heavy, not at all pleased.

"No," Nakajima said crisply, shaking his head.

"Then what do you mean?" I asked.

And Nakajima answered. "That's just how it has to be. Because I can live with you, even though I can't live with anyone else. And I'm tired of always being by myself. I'm tired of sleeping alone, with that wire rack under my arm. Now that I know what it's like not to be on my own, I can't go back to living the way I was before."

"Somehow it's not much fun when you lay it all out like that," I said. "Paris, huh? I would like to go sometime, only right now I'm really enjoying my work a lot, you know?"

"You don't have another job scheduled yet, do you?" Nakajima asked.

"No. There are a few possibilities, but none of them seem to be in a rush."

"What's the problem, then?" Nakajima said. "Do you really need to be in Japan now, at this moment in your life, at this exact moment in your life?"

He had a point. I wasn't particularly interested in Paris, but I did like the idea of being able to spend several days going through the Louvre from start to finish, since I'd only been there for about an hour once with my mom. I hadn't seen Versailles yet, either.

And now that my mom was gone, there was nothing to keep me in Japan.

A flood of loneliness hit me the second I realized that.

I wanted my mom to be alive, tying me down. To be showing her disapproval, telling me, *I don't know, going abroad?—it's so far, and we won't be able to see each other.* I yearned to hear those words, to hear her saying them. But I never would again.

"That's true, I guess."

"This idea that you have to stay—that's how people think when they have a family, and it's located in some fixed place, whereas you and I..."

Having said this much of something huge, Nakajima fell silent.

The way he broke off suggested he had said as much as he could, as much as he wanted to. I was used to this by now. I didn't know where it came from, but I had grasped the outlines.

After a long pause, he continued. "I think it'd be great if we could share an apartment, and meals. Since this is my idea, we don't even have to go halvsies. I'll cover what you can't."

"Halvsies. I haven't heard that word in a while," I said, changing the topic for a moment. Then, "I have the money my mom left me, so I think I could probably afford it. I'm sure my dad would help out, too."

Nakajima nodded. "After all, when your mom passed away, your dad inherited that club of hers, right? You have every right to ask him for a little money. Sometimes asking a favor is the best way to show your love, don't you think?"

He had a point there, too, though I'd been trying not to think about that.

"You're too cavalier about money, Chihiro. Just not in the usual way."

It tickled me to have Nakajima lecturing me on practical matters. I grinned.

Lately, he was starting to speak more and more freely, in words that came from deep inside him. And that made me happy.

I'd do anything to help him keep moving in that direction. I was even willing to go see my dad, and be pleasant.

One afternoon, my good buddy Yotchan came over to the wall with his friend Miki to bring me a snack. Rice crackers, potato chips, and chocolate.

"See, with all this color they're not ghosts anymore, are they?" I said.

The design was almost finished, and I spent my days staring at it, adding a bit of color here and there and redoing parts to make it more balanced. I was at the stage when all the different parts gradually begin to come together, to form a world of their own.

"Poor ghosts," Yotchan said. "They still look lonely."

"Don't talk like that! You're scaring me!" Miki cried. "I hate ghosts."

"Even if they're monkeys?" I asked.

I guess even with the color, their loneliness still shines through.
"Yeah."

"I've never seen a real lake," Yotchan said.

"I have. I saw Lake Ashi," Miki said.

I listened to their conversation, marveling at its novelty. At the same time, I was thinking to myself that I had failed, they still looked like ghosts. The kids could see that somehow they were different from the other monkeys. Although if I was able to express those kinds of things, maybe I wasn't such a bad painter after all....

After that, Yotchan and Miki started talking about some TV show, and I went on painting in the colors. They were in the way, but even so I was glad they had come.

When I glanced back, they were squatting down eating the snacks they had brought, along with some *manjū* Sayuri had handed out, chattering back and forth. I took a swig of hot herbal tea from my thermos and tried to think of some way I could capture the brilliance of their exchanges, the colors that glittered in their words.

My butt felt cold from sitting on the ground and my sides hurt from having my arms up in the air for so long, but I couldn't stop painting.

With each color I added, another rose up before me, and I would keep chasing them, one after the other, until the sun set and I couldn't paint anymore, and then I'd go home and sleep like a log.

Now when I thought of home, Nakajima was part of the picture. He was always studying, and always stayed in my apartment, whether or not I was there. *I guess he really must want to be with me.* He came over because he wanted to. I could believe that, I felt, more than I ever could have with anyone else.

Wherever Nakajima is, that's the place I go home to. That's what lets me go all day without thinking about anything. About what I'm going to do with my life, stuff like that.

Eventually the kids left, and I was taking a break, pleased with the progress I'd made today, when Sayuri appeared, making a beeline for me, her expression glum.

She'd always smiled and waved when I saw her before, so I waited, wondering what was up.

"Do you have a minute, Chihiro?" she said.

"Doesn't look like it's good news," I said.

They must have decided to tear down the center, I thought, even with the mural here.

In fact, it was a somewhat trickier problem. Something that gave me pause.

"We got a call from the district mayor, he says they've got a sponsor."

"A sponsor? But I thought the district was paying for this!"

"The thing is, they were talking things over, and apparently this sponsor says that if it will help energize the district he's willing to assume the entire cost."

"That's odd. It doesn't seem necessary at this point," I said.

Sayuri nodded. "I know. The catch is that he wants you to work his company's logo into the picture somehow, as big as possible. You know that sign on the roof of the huge *kon'nyaku* factory near the turnoff for the highway? That's it."

Sayuri showed me a picture. It was the most bizarre logo you could imagine: an incredibly ugly combination of colors, mostly gray, with the company mascot in the middle. The mascot was a block of *kon'nyaku* with a smiley face.

"Oh, my god!" I laughed. "You've got to be kidding!"

Sayuri burst out laughing, too.

We were both well aware that in this society, things you'd

think could only be bad jokes actually happen all the time. And so, wiping away a few tears after my laughter had subsided, I told her, "There's no way. I mean, I've practically finished the design."

Even as I spoke, I was trying to think of some way to incorporate a humorous take on the logo into the mural, but it really didn't seem possible.

And I had a sneaking suspicion that even if it were possible, the sponsor wouldn't like it if I made a joke of his logo.

"At any rate, I'll try and negotiate," Sayuri said. "Don't lose hope."

This sounded like it could get annoying.

"Listen, why don't I just quit, someone else can finish it. With the logo," I suggested. "Or you can find someone to design a whole new picture around the logo."

"Why do you always have to be so absolute about things?" Sayuri said, stunned.

So I had to try again. "How about this, then: I'll have to put the name of the district in as a sponsor over my signature, so why don't just we add the logo there, too, very small?"

"The president of the company wants it bigger, as part of the picture," Sayuri said. "But if it's going to end up being an ad, there's really no point in having you paint it. Right now I'm threatening them, telling them it will cost a million yen to redo the whole picture."

Sayuri grinned.

I like her when she's like that, so I tried to be as gentle as I could, so that I wouldn't sound like I was just being picky. "To tell the truth, I don't think my pictures are particularly great. And I've been painting this one knowing that it might well be destroyed sometime in the not-too-distant future. But there's a huge difference between *not* saying you *won't* paint anything because it might be destroyed and saying sure, anything goes because it might be destroyed. I may not be much of a painter, but I don't just do any old thing, like someone doing hand-painted movie posters. Whenever someone offers me a job, I only take it under the condition that I can paint what I want—and I think I'm able, maybe only barely able but still able, to create murals that justify that freedom. So for someone to come along, just like that, and ... it doesn't matter what it is, no matter how cute the *kon'nyaku* character is, or if it's Pikachu or Gandam or Hamtaro—I don't care, if someone is telling me to put something like that into a mural of mine, it means they didn't understand my work when they hired me."

"I understand that, I really do. That's the whole reason I wanted you to take this on, and I take full responsibility for everything that's happening, so you don't have to worry. I just came to fill you in, not to try to persuade you."

Like the good teacher she was, Sayuri kept calm and inspired trust.

"At any rate, if this turns out to be an inflexible demand,

I can't do it, I can't work in a system like that," I said. "It's totally wrong. They're asking the wrong person. Tell them they ought to ask a sign-painter for stuff like that. I'm not disrespecting sign painters, by the way—it's just a different profession. I know I'm only a step or two above an amateur, but I can't switch professions for something like this."

I looked at the mural. Poor monkeys. You may end up being painted over, painted out of existence. But who knows? Maybe Yotchan and his friends will remember that you were here, even if only for a short time.

The thought liberated me. I felt as if the things I'd been clinging to were crumbling, blowing away in the wind, dispersing. Leaving me free to go anywhere I wanted.

This is nice, I thought, really nice.

I figured I might as well take a picture, anyway, and snapped a shot with my digital camera, with the sky as the background. To preserve the joy of this special stage in the painting.

"I'm sure there's a way," Sayuri said. "For starters, I'm planning to show the video of that TV program you were in to the people in the mayor's office, and from the company. I'll try and make them see how valuable this is as art."

"Kind of embarrassing, considering the quality of my work," I said.

For the first time, though, I was beginning to take what I was doing a tiny bit seriously.

It was hard to say for sure since the president of the company hadn't seen the mural yet, but I had to acknowledge that some of the responsibility for what might happen lay with me. I just wasn't good enough to paint a picture no one would want to mess up with a logo.

It'd be nice to study painting more, to see all kinds of really, really incredible artworks and realize just how minuscule I am.... All on its own, the path to Paris was opening up before me. I pictured Nakajima in profile, engrossed in his studies at home.

I wanted to be able to have that same look on my face when I painted. Not to run away from everything that had happened in a day, but to turn it all into another form of energy, make it part of myself. That's how I wanted my painting to be.

But first I'd have to finish what I had started here.

"Okay, and I'll do my best to get featured in a magazine or something, to make myself at least a little more visible," I said. "Middle-aged men are impressed by that kind of thing, right? And I can ask the professor who advised me on my thesis project to write the mayor a letter—she's a pretty well-known artist, and she's from the area, so I bet her opinion will carry a lot of weight. She's the one who did that weird bronze sculpture in front of the train station, I think. And on top of that, I'll send a letter to the president of the company, along with some materials about the mural, making it as conciliatory and pleasant as possible, to try and bring him around. If that doesn't work, we'll just have to give up."

I thought it was a splendid plan. Unless he were incredibly wealthy and eccentric, the president probably wouldn't want to pay to have me erase a mural I had gone to all the trouble of painting and then do another one. I felt confident it would work.

"I bet that'll do the trick," Sayuri said. "I'm sorry, putting you to so much trouble."

"That's okay. I'll give it a try."

After all, I thought, maybe this will be my last job in Japan. I wasn't necessarily determined to go on working as a muralist, so I really had no idea what the future might hold.

Things like this were bound to happen no matter what kind of life I ended up leading, and whether they turned out well or badly, I'd just have to do my best, the way I would this time. And inhale the sweet scent of the freedom I'd earned when it came wafting over.

"Let me know when something's been decided," I said. "I'll take a break until then, once I get to a stopping place. It's okay, I know it's not your fault."

I had things to do, and I needed to cool down, and it made me sad to look at the picture when it was so close to being done, so I hurriedly packed up my stuff.

Of course I wasn't angry. I felt bad for Sayuri, actually.

It was only natural that they felt entitled to order me

around—it's not like I was a famous artist or anything. And I'm not a particularly imposing person, either: they probably assumed I'd just go right along with their request that I work an ad into my painting. I saw that.

In a way, it really made sense. That kind of willingness to give in is rampant in this society of ours. From banks to *ponzu* sauce ... well, those are just examples. The point is that people have found a gazillion little opportunities to profit in questionable ways, all over the place. I've seen tons of cases, all across the board, where in order to grab on to those tiny profits people studiously adopt another perspective, keeping their true opinions to themselves, and no one takes responsibility, everyone just huddles together on some middle ground, and it all gets less and less clear, yet in the end everyone ends up being crammed into a rigid, unyielding framework. I've seen the same story play out over and over again.

But I couldn't take it. The whole dumb setup just bored me to death.

Here I am playing nicely with the world, trying my best to leave things the tiniest bit better than they were, trying to fly even a little bit higher—how annoying it would be to have to go along with this crap. That was my take on it.

If I were Sayuri, for instance, and the Infant Development Center mattered more to me than anything else, and if I were part of the organization, I'm sure I could have found all kinds of solutions to their problems, and I would have gone with the policy that was best for everyone.

But in the current situation, going along with this new proposal would have gone against the essence of my profession. If I were a stranger passing through this district and I happened to see this wall and the ad were part of the mural, I'd think it was pathetic. Besides, I have to say I don't think much of a company that feels it has to have its name plastered all over the place simply because it's shelling out five hundred thousand yen.

Right now five hundred thousand yen is a huge amount of money to me, but that doesn't mean I'll just do whatever it takes to be paid. Especially not something like abandoning my professional standards, because that would throw the rest of my life out of balance.

All this reminded me of an incident involving a sculptor I respect.

This sculptor had been asked to create a sculpture for a plaza in a certain town in Europe. In the place where the plaza then stood there had once been a forest inhabited by gypsies, large numbers of whom had died during some war. So he suggested he make a statue showing gypsies. He was thinking of all the terrible discrimination gypsies have suffered. An open area like the plaza was, he thought, the perfect place to commemorate a population that had been subjected to the evils of the human spirit, whose true story had always been concealed, consigned to oblivion. But the mayor and the citizens of the town refused to go along—there were still gypsies, they said, who grabbed purses and picked pockets and generally made themselves a nuisance to tourists—people like them didn't deserve to be celebrated with a statue. And so the whole project was indefinitely put on hold.

That's how it goes. Things look different depending on your perspective.

As I see it, fighting to bridge those gaps isn't what really matters. The most important thing is to know them inside and out, as differences, and to understand why certain people are the way they are.

My job was to insist on my own perspective, right to the end, and in order to do that I needed to brush up on my technique. However famous you may be, these disagreements are bound to continue, and ultimately it doesn't really matter that I'm not that much of a painter.

Well, maybe it does. If I had more confidence, it'd be easier to hold my own.

That's the crucial thing.

The truth, sad to say, is that I still can't declare with any real conviction that the people of this town would be better off with my mural on the wall rather than that goofy logo. That's the problem, I thought with a twinge of shame: I'm still too young, too green.

Returning early to the apartment, I found Nakajima studying madly, his PowerBook open and a dictionary in his hand.

"Early, aren't you?" he said.

"I got stuff for dinner," I said. "No need to make anything."

I didn't particularly need to say that, but that's what came out.

"Oh? I was looking forward to making dinner again today. It's a nice way to take a break," Nakajima said. "How about I go and get us some coffee from that place where they roast the beans themselves? It would be nice to talk a walk." Then, looking me in the face for the first time, "Oh, looks like something bad happened today."

I nodded and told him what had happened.

"Yeah, it's not surprising, given your low level of celebrity and how unsophisticated people are in that part of the city," Nakajima said.

"You don't mince words, do you?" I said, impressed.

"If you don't say what you're thinking, you end up lying when you really need to speak up," Nakajima said.

"Anyhow, I can't draw a stupid *kon'nyaku* logo into my picture. I just can't."

"Did you see what it looks like?"

"I did. It's this *kon'nyaku* mascot with a weird blob of words above it. *Very* uncool."

"Could you stick it in a corner somewhere, really small?"

"That would be fine with me, but the sponsor said it has to be big."

"That's something they would have had to make clear from the beginning."

"You're telling me."

"And even if your picture is still a work in progress, it's like a sapling that will eventually grow into a huge tree or something—it has that kind of glow. They've got to see that."

"More plain speaking from Nakajima ... I mean, even I don't see that kind of value in my murals yet. That's why I have no problem painting in a place that could be torn down."

"I know, but your modest assessment of your own worth and the decision to treat your work like a billboard are two totally different things."

"I'm with you there."

"Besides, they hired you to do a job. They can't keep changing their minds about what that job is."

"Exactly."

"How about telling them you'll quit unless they agree to have the logo at the edge, very small?"

"That's what I thought."

"Do you have any connections? Professors at the art school, say, or some famous art critic?"

"A few."

"Have them say something. It helps to fight authority with

authority, I think. And if you could get someone to come do a story about your work, write an article that would give meaning to your mural or something, that would make your position stronger, too. And if you should end up in court or something, who cares? Sayuri can decide for herself where she stands." Nakajima paused a moment, then continued. "See, people like us are never at the center of things. We're always on the margins, and I generally figure it's best not to stand out too much. Most of the time we see things in exactly the opposite light as the majority does, and people don't look kindly on you if you stand out. When push comes to shove, though, you've got to have something you won't cave in on. Otherwise, you end up like a recluse or something, cut off from the world."

Our opinions were so close I felt as if he were reading my mind.

The amazing alignment of our perspectives made me forget how annoyed I'd been at the prospect of having to stop painting and go to all this trouble doing irrelevant things. That feeling faded so quickly it was like magic.

When something unpleasant happened during the day, I used to come home and pet my cat to cheer myself up. Being with Nakajima seemed to have a similar effect, neutralizing the poison that had accumulated inside me.

My old self would probably have come in without saying a word and tried to forget it all by having sex with whoever

I was sleeping with just then, not talking to him about what had happened, keeping everything bottled up inside. That shows you how much respect I had for my lovers.

But Nakajima was different, I thought. This time it was for real.

At this very moment, I was truly beginning to fall in love. It weighed on me and it was sometimes a pain in the ass, but the payoff could be big, too. So big it felt like gazing up into the sky. Or like looking out an airplane window at the ocean, with clouds shining above it.

It was so gorgeous it almost felt like sadness.

Like the feeling you get when you realize that, in the grand scheme of things, your time here on this earth really isn't all that long after all.

There was one other thing I had to do.

"Hey, Dad, I'm at the station now. Do you have some time today?"

I didn't want to call him at work, so I'd called his cell phone.

"Wow, this is sudden," my dad said.

"Well, the job I had scheduled sort of stopped unexpectedly," I replied. "It's hard for me to get out here unless something like that happens."

"I can get away for a while in the evening," my dad said. "We could have dinner in about two hours."

The restaurant my dad chose was this incredibly mediocre Italian place, and whenever he went there his Prominent Local Personage thing went into high gear. I couldn't stand it.

But I'd asked to see him without any warning, and of course he'd be treating me, so I figured I had no right to complain.

With a family as stable as mine had been, my heart certainly wasn't scarred, or if it was, the scars were ones I'd made myself—now that I was comparing myself to Nakajima all the time I could see that. I thought I was pretty tough, too. Still, I cried a bit at the station.

The days I'd passed with my mom before she died were still there, it seemed, seared into the corners of my heart.

The atmosphere of the station brought it all back. I could see myself running to the hospital, glad to be seeing my mother again. You never know you're happy until later. Because physical sensations like smells and exhaustion don't figure into our memories, I guess. Only the good bits bob up into view.

I was always startled by the snatches of memory that I saw as happy, how they came.

This time, it was the feeling I got when I stepped out onto the platform. The sense of what it had been like to be on my way to see my mom, for her still to be alive, if only for the time being, if only for that day. The happiness of that knowledge had come back to life inside me.

And the loneliness of that moment. The helplessness.

The fact that now when I came to this station, I could go see my dad, but not my mom. I'd always done that in the past, but now I couldn't.

"You know, the chef in this place spent four whole years in Italy! Seriously. Hey, kid, do me a favor and ask Sugiyama to come say hi when he has a moment, will you? I want to introduce him to my daughter."

Just as I expected: he'd said it. In my heart I was thinking, *Please, I've already heard that story, and how could he "have a moment" when he's got a restaurant full of customers?* But I kept quiet.

Before long a man in a tall chef's hat came out and talked for a while with my dad, and he said hello to me, too, so I just kept smiling away.

I'd be leaving Japan soon, after all, and probably wouldn't be seeing my dad for a while. When I thought about that, I felt kind of attached even to his preening.

After that the dishes started coming out: huge quantities of pasta that had obviously been boiled too long, especially considering that the chef had lived in Italy for four years, and tiny servings of the main courses. I suppose he must have ended up adapting to the tastes of his customers out here in the country—he didn't have any choice. I'd met some exchange students from Italy when I was in art school, and I had made a few super-low-budget trips to the towns they had come from. Needless to say, none of the restaurants in Italy had been as half-hearted in their approach as this one.

As I thought back fondly over those days, I began to realize with more and more clarity that I was seriously on the verge of going to Europe. And I was going there *for myself.*

"Listen, Dad," I said. "I'm thinking of going to study in Paris next year."

"With a guy, I take it?" He didn't miss a beat.

I was stunned.

"What makes you think that?" I asked.

"I can see it in your face," he replied. "You look ready to be a mom."

"Do I?"

I smiled. Maybe I was more giddy than I realized.

"Anyway, it sounds good to me. It's great you're even able to consider it. Bring him to see me before you go, though, will you?"

"Well, if I can," I said. "You'll have to wait a bit."

Nakajima was too weird, not the kind of guy you introduce to your family.

"What does he do?" my dad asked. "Don't tell me he wants to be a painter."

"No."

"He's younger than you? A student?" my dad said.

I was impressed at how close to the truth he was. Parents are amazing.

"He's in med school. We're the same age, but he is a student. He wants to get a scholarship to study at this research institute in Paris when he finishes his degree."

"I suspected there was a man behind this. Can't say I like it. Not a bit."

He seemed genuinely displeased.

"Terrible, getting me to confess it all." I smiled.

"Well, once you've settled on an art school in Paris, send me a breakdown of all the funds you'll need. And promise you'll come visit me sometimes."

"Oh, I won't need anything—I've got the money Mom left," I said. "And you don't have to give me anything to get me to come visit. Of course I'll come! You should come see me in Paris, too. And to tell the truth, you're the only one I want to see. I'd rather not have to see your relatives anymore, honestly."

"No, I don't like it when you have to spend time with my sister and the rest of that crowd, either," my dad said. "I hate seeing you unhappy. But please—if I do send you some money, don't turn it down, okay? And if anything should happen, let me know. Definitely. If you get hurt, or pregnant, or you break up with this guy and start living on your own, or you quit school ... any big change. Tell me. And if you can manage it, introduce him. Anytime is fine."

"Okay."

Thank you, Dad, I thought, chewing my mushy pasta.

My relationship with him had entered a new phase.

You don't necessarily have to *want* to become an adult; it happens as a matter of course, as you go, making choices. The important thing, I think, is to choose for yourself.

Standing next to my dad, I realized that his body no longer smelled like a middle-aged man's. All of a sudden, he smelled like a grandfather.

That's what happens when you live apart.

We'll probably never live under the same roof again. The second that thought struck me, days that had seemed utterly unremarkable were made irreplaceable, unforgettable. I came face-to-face, once more, with a time I had left behind. My dad had been part of the life I'd lived then, he was woven indistinguishably into the fabric, with exactly the same color thread.

But life keeps flowing on. Maybe if his business failed and he went bankrupt and everyone in this town abandoned him, he and I might end up living near each other. If I were somehow to become extraordinarily wealthy, say, and I rented an apartment for him to live in. There was no way that would happen, I knew that, but daydreaming alleviated my jealousy.

The jealousy I felt, after my mom died, at losing my dad to this town.

Deep inside me, the child I used to be is crying. *Weren't you supposed to drop everything else and just be my dad, after Mom died? How can you go on running the same company, as if nothing has happened, and go on hanging out with those relatives of yours? What did all the time we spent together as a family mean to you? Was it just a game for you, playing at our being a family?*

But the adult I've become wants her freedom, and the truth is that I wouldn't like it at all if my dad actually thrust himself into my life.

And so, like a man and a woman secretly in love, we remain silent about the half-wish we each feel, that somehow we could live together.

I guess this is one way to love, I think.

Love isn't only a matter of fussing over each other, hugging, wanting to be together. Some things communicate, inevitably, precisely because you keep them in check. The heartfelt feelings that find their way to you in the form of money and imported gourmet ham.

Having the sensitivity to gauge those things is a real gift.

Our negotiating strategies seemed to have worked, because things went well.

I managed to have the interview take place just in time to meet the deadline for a certain magazine's next issue. The timing was perfect: people who saw the article started coming to watch while I was still working on the mural, and the fact that it was featured in a magazine seems to have convinced people in the neighborhood that my work must have value, even if did look like a child's doodling.

The letter I'd written and the recommendation from my art school professor had been delivered to the president of the *kon'nyaku* company, and he'd come to take a look at the site where I was painting the mural. He was extremely pleased to see it was the center of so much activity, and he decided that it would be a shame to ruin the picture; it would be good enough just to put the logo somewhere at the edge. I lucked out because he was a pleasant man: he had broad shoulders, and looked sort of like a block of *kon'nyaku* himself. He asked me to mention the company when the local newspaper and a cable TV station came to interview me after the mural was completed.

I didn't really care one way or the other as long as the picture could be saved, so naturally I smiled good-naturedly and agreed. Sayuri, who had gotten the knack of managing things like this through the process of negotiating and arranging my painting schedule and so on, told me that if she ever lost her job she would come and be my agent.

"So it looks like I'll be able to finish the mural after all. Everything went beautifully. Thanks again, Nakajima. I really appreciate your standing by me," I said.

We were at a homey *teishoku* restaurant near the apartment. I was having ginger pork.

"So it worked, that's great! I figured it would. We're surrounded by all these bozos who don't know the difference between a mural and an advertisement, after all. They're bound to have a weakness for mass media stars."

There he goes again, being a bit *too* frank.

Something in his bluntness reminded me of Chii.

"I bet that's true anywhere, no matter what country you're in," I said.

"I'm not so sure about that," Nakajima replied, taking a bite of his boiled mackerel set. "It might be easier if you were dealing with people who see historically significant architecture and incredible paintings on church ceilings and so on every day. I don't know much about art, so I really have no idea how great those things are, but I'm really looking forward to seeing a lot once we're in Paris. I get the feeling that in countries with that kind of history, even researchers will take a different attitude toward their work—just thinking about it makes my heart pound. I won't even be able to compete, I bet, in all kinds of areas."

"I feel the same way," I said. "In Paris, I'll be able to spend as much time as I want looking at paintings of the sort I'd have to line up to see for just fifteen seconds at the museums in Ueno Park. There's simply no comparison in the quantity of what's available. And I'll be able to see as many paintings in churches as I want. After all, I'm most interested in frescos.... If I have a chance, I'd love to learn about restoration, too—there's so much I want to do! It's all there for me to study, from now on. I owe that to you: it's only after we met that I've started wanting so badly to go and learn more about the things I'm interested in."

The restaurant was packed with students and single men; there was a baseball game on TV. Waiters bustled back and forth, calling out one order after another. We hardly ever ate out, so it all seemed very novel. I felt dazzled looking at everyone, like a mole fresh out of its tunnel.

I had suggested to Nakajima that I take him out to eat, even though we never ate out, because I wanted to thank him for being there for me during my troubles with the mural. He grudgingly came along, saying that maybe it would be nice to go out for a change.

Having dinner at a local *teishoku* place, for the first time in ages ... that's all we were doing. Back when I was on my own, this scene would have been drearily familiar. But since every little opinion Nakajima offered was linked to a whole other universe, the ordinariness of it all melted away, affording me glimpses of the unknown.

"The thing that concerns me," Nakajima said, "is that

people might start offering you lots more jobs now that you're getting a little more famous, and then you won't be interested in going to Paris anymore."

He kept his eyes down as he said this. He carefully picked the small clams out of his miso soup, one at a time, and popped them into his mouth.

"If I did get offered a job, I'd certainly go anywhere in Japan to do it, as long as that were possible, right until the last minute. I want to earn money that way as long as I can," I said. "But I'm going to Paris. My life with you is important to me, and I want to be overwhelmed, too, while I'm still not too old. I want to be blown away by greatness. Because I've started wanting to become a better person, now, even just a little bit better."

"I'm glad of that," Nakajima said.

He had a habit, when he was truly happy, of not showing it.

We sound like a married couple, I thought.

Playing at marriage, playing at being a dad, playing at being a full member of society.

Everything in my life revolves around people *playing* at being something.

But that's only because we have to be that way in order to get on with our lives. Just because people are playing doesn't mean their hearts aren't in it.

The schedule was pretty tight, and I ended up staying pretty late a few times, but at last I finished the mural.

Sayuri and the center's director and I took a photo to mark the occasion, and, as promised, I made a special point of highlighting the name of the *kon'nyaku* company and thanking it for its support in an interview with the local paper and on TV. We took another picture with the children from the center, with whom I'd become good friends, as if we had all gone camping together or something, and then they took me to a *yakiniku* place to celebrate.

After it was all over, in the middle of the night, I climbed over the gate and snuck onto the grounds all alone, and went to stand in front of the mural.

Maybe it was because I'd just finished it, but it looked really terrific. It was the best of all my works to date. There was a boldness to it that defied the darkness, even when no one was there to see it.

At last, a faint sense of confidence dropped anchor inside me.

Now, I thought, *I'm free to leave.*

The monkeys in the picture dashed around like they had no time to waste. Little blasts of color radiated out, one overlapping with another, merging, like a rainbow.

And then my eye landed on those two monkeys, one drinking tea and one in her bed, and something inside me shimmered.

Maybe I should go see them. By myself ... yeah, I'll go see Mino and his sister.

I'd take along a picture of this mural to show them, and talk to Chii.

I was trying to remember what train line we had taken, where we changed, what that lake had been called, when all of a sudden I remembered what Yotchan had said.

Ghosts.

And I began to wonder.

Maybe that place never existed, it was all a figment of Nakajima's imagination. Could it be that the two of them, Mino and Chii, were no longer living? That Yotchan had been right?

I shuddered. That seemed so much more likely than that it had been real.

I'm a pretty practical person, and ordinarily there's no way I'd even consider such a thing, but ... somehow the notion seemed oddly right. I felt like I was lost, body and all, in a fog of memories, and the feeling refused to dissipate. Nakajima had the power to make you lose sight of the boundary between what you had actually experienced and what you hadn't—maybe it wasn't real, after all. Maybe in the end Nakajima's whole existence was aiming somewhere else, not toward the light but away from it. I got that feeling somehow.

I was comfortable with him, and to a certain degree I was in love, so it hadn't bothered me, but I couldn't help noticing that there was something in him that scared me every so often.

Or maybe that's necessary when two people are serious about each other?

We try our hardest not to feel that, to sweep it under the carpet, but I bet it's there.

A particular variety of loneliness, like peering deep into the darkness.

It's only natural, when two separate universes touch.

For instance, when I was a child I saw a lot of vomit, middle-aged women totally drunk with their bras cutting into the flesh of their backs, and even middle-aged men running their eyes lasciviously over my young body—I was used to it. And that was only the beginning.... It wasn't hard for me to imagine a world out there in which murder was an everyday occurrence. That wasn't *my* world, and it wasn't the world my parents had lived in, but somewhere, anywhere, all you had to do was peel away the skin, and you'd discover a path leading down into it.

Everyone knows that hidden pull is there, but we go on living our lives, pretending we don't. We keep our gazes fixed, day after day, on the things we want to see.

But sometimes we encounter people like Nakajima who compel us to remember it *all*. He doesn't have to say or do anything in particular; just looking at him, you find yourself face-to-face with the enormousness of the world as a whole.

Because he doesn't try to live in just a part of it. Because he doesn't avert his gaze.

He makes me feel like I've suddenly awakened, and I want to go on watching him forever. That, I think, is what it is. I'm awed by his terrible depths.

A few days later, in the morning, I set out for that town.

Stepping down from the train alone this time, the station seemed even more forlorn than it had the first time. The only sign of life in the dead of the afternoon was the supermarket, whose huge electric sign glowed. It seemed to suck people in: elderly men and women, prematurely aged housewives.

I kept walking on and on along the single street that extended from the station and found the road that led to the lake. The breeze carried the scent of water. Passing a small boathouse, a run-down shop that sold fishing tackle, and a closed restaurant, I emerged from the woods onto the shore of the lake.

I cared for Nakajima so deeply that I was shaking. I felt it even more in his absence.

Last time, when we had walked here together, the lake had been more beautiful than it was now, and shone more brilliantly. I guess I must have been in love already.

The lake, utterly still now, seemed to have been abandoned

by the world and its goings-on. There was no mist yet; the sunlight beat down almost painfully on the bare tree branches.

I kept walking, heading for the red *torii*. My footsteps were uncertain, as if I were walking in a dream. *What if it's just a ruin when I get there, empty for the past hundred years?* I thought. I wouldn't have been surprised if it were.

So I was relieved when the small house came into view. Relieved, and stunned.

Because Mino was standing in the doorway, waving.

I ran over. "How on earth..." I said.

"Chii said you'd be coming, alone this time," Mino said. "I was out here waiting."

"It's amazing she knows these things," I said. "And that you would have such faith in her that you'd come out and wait for me, like a little dog or something."

Without thinking, I patted Mino on the head. He had the most adorably dog-like round eyes to begin with, and for him to be perched on the stoop like this ... it was so cute I could hardly stand it.

"I'm *not* a dog." Mino smiled. "Come on inside. I'll make us some tea."

I smiled back and followed him through the door.

Relief washed over me. *They exist. It wasn't a dream.*

If anything, it was Nakajima's bizarre mood that had made them seem unreal.

The house was just as tidy as before, and yet it felt homey. Somehow you always get that sense when you visit someplace for the second time, and that's how it was here, too. This was a place I could relax in. And now I knew my way around.

I sat back and watched Mino as he boiled water and made tea. There wasn't anything unusual about the way he did these things, but his movements were very precise. He took his time, but he wasn't dawdling. It was like watching a master at the tea ceremony.

"It's no use trying to steal my technique. It's all in the spring water."

Mino smiled.

"Maybe I'll take some when I go."

"I'll show you where later," Mino said.

The tea, made from leaves with a subtly smoky aroma, was so good I could feel my senses sharpening. It had a sweetness to it, and at the end of each sip I'd catch a whiff of fruit.

"It's delicious. . . ." I murmured.

"Life sure is funny," Mino said. "Ordinarily I don't go out much—I order most of what we need, books and tea leaves and so on, online. The supermarket in front of the station is really the only place I go. The weird thing is, while I never feel any desire to see other people, I get all happy when someone tells me they like the tea I make."

"Maybe you just know I recognize good tea when I drink it?" I said.

"That could be," Mino said.

I sort of knew what he meant.

I'm sure that if I hadn't been a friend of Nakajima's, if I were a traveler who just happened to run into Mino on the road, or a tourist in the area who randomly dropped by this shack, he wouldn't have opened his heart to me the way he did. We wouldn't have been able to talk this intimately.

Mino and Nakajima were a lot alike in that way.

They weren't casual about things the way normal people are. They didn't see any reason to try and be amiable with people just because they happened to be there.

Maybe in a sense their way of doing things was kind of sad, but it put me at ease. Because it's *normal*.

In most cases, relationships fall into place the second you figure out who someone is and once you have a grasp of the context that led to your meeting them. For Mino and Nakajima, though, that process was all messed up.

Think of those kids at the center. They're honest but cautious; they would never come plop themselves down beside me and start asking questions right from the first day. It always takes at least a week before kids start pestering me and getting excited.

I've got more experience with life than they do, it's true, and sometimes as I paint I start thinking, *Look, ultimately we're going to get friendly anyway, and once I finish painting I'll be gone. So why don't you hurry up and come over? What's the point in waiting?*

But just because you're working within a fixed time frame like that doesn't mean you can just leap over the distance that separates you. The kids, in this case, are right.

I could relax with Mino because he didn't seem to have any extra baggage, and I sensed that over time, little by little, we would become friendly. It was the same as with the kids.

It's more than just a matter of words—there's always a physical distance to overcome. We look each other in the eye, smell the air, drink our tea together, gathering up tiny sparks of reassurance. And then there's the matter of affinity. If Nakajima had attempted to decrease the distance between us two weeks earlier than he had, I bet I would have been turned off. I probably never would have cried as I had, touched at the sight of his wire rack.

"I feel like this could become a habit—taking the train here, making my way around the lake, coming here for a delicious cup of tea," I said. "Would it be all right if I visited occasionally, Mino, with Nakajima? Not to have my fortune told, just to come."

"Yes," Mino said quietly. "Maybe then our stopped time would move again."

The stopped time, I realized, was Nakajima's, too.

"Quite a hero, aren't you?" Mino said in Chii's voice. Mino's eyes were closed.

Chii's eyes, too, were closed. She was asleep, breathing lightly, her chest rising and falling slightly under the fluffy comforter that covered her.

"Wouldn't I be a heroine?"

This time, no longer unnerved by her sarcasm, I could be myself.

I could totally see why Nakajima had wanted to see them so badly. Basically, they were really nice, interesting people. They had managed to build something like a solid, healthy household on a foundation that was seriously skewed. Here, keeping to themselves, they treasured certain elements of life, like restraint and dignity, that people in the city had long since abandoned.

"No, Nobu's the heroine of the story," Chii said. "The damsel in distress. You saved him from the prison he'd shut himself up inside, you woke him up and brought him out."

I sort of knew what she meant.

"Go to Paris with him. You two may well end up living there for quite some time, but do it anyway," Chii said. "You seem to be hesitating, but isn't it too late for that? He's grabbed you. And you've grabbed him, too—he can't live by himself anymore. I think I can show you an image that will make you understand. Here, give me your hand."

Looking at Chii, I saw that she had opened her eyes. The

color of her eyes was so deep I shuddered. I didn't want to touch her, but I figured that was just my instincts telling me to steer clear of anything too powerful. And since I had come this far, why not? Screwing up my courage, I took her hand in mine. It was smooth, and very thin. The hand of a sleeping beauty who had nothing to do with ordinary life.

"Close your eyes," Chii said. "Match your breathing with mine. It seems like hypnotism, I know, and in a way it's sort of similar, but it's not hypnotism. We're simply going to share an image. Don't be afraid."

I did just as she told me. The dark screen in front of my eyes was blank. But after a while, as I waited, absolutely still, an image rose up in my mind. All at once, just like that.

It was snowing.... In a dark sky, like motes of dust, like bird feathers pirouetting in the air, ever so lightly, snow was drifting this way and that.

I was looking down on the snow from above. I could tell because the flakes kept tumbling away from me. Then, all of a sudden, I was up in a tree somewhere, watching the street below. Gradually, I realized that the tree was just one in a row that lined the street. It was an ordinary paved street; no sooner had the snowflakes landed on it than they melted. The only place they were starting to pile up, in a thin layer, was on the roofs of the cars parked along the street.

I saw Nakajima in the distance, walking toward me, a heavy-looking backpack full of books on his shoulder. I could tell it had books in it because of the neat, square way it bulged.

Hey, it's Nakajima! Just look at him, he's so cool! I thought automatically. *The way he stoops over like that, the long toes in those shoes of his*—I love it all. It's not logical.

Looking more closely as he approached, I noticed that he seemed to have lost weight and he looked pale and unsteady on his feet. He must have been studying nonstop again, without taking a break to eat. As if he were trying, by studying, to free himself from something. Then, without any warning, he stopped and looked up.

I doubt our eyes could have met then, since I was transparent.

He slumped down on the ground and leaned against the tree. There was no one else around, just the snow dancing lightly in the air. Nakajima was watching the snow. His eyes were lovely. His face wore the expression of someone confronted by something wonderful.

Then Nakajima opened his backpack and slipped an object awkwardly out from between the books that did, indeed, fill the backpack almost to the bursting point. It was that old wire rack. He put it under his arm like a thermometer and closed his eyes.

"No! Don't go to sleep there! You'll freeze!" I screamed.

The sound of my own screaming jolted me into consciousness.

Chii was still holding my hand, her eyes open. She was watching me.

Once again Mino spoke in Chii's voice. "That was a symbolic representation of Nobu's past, and of his future. Of what happened to him, and what could happen again."

"I can't allow that," I said, tears welling unexpectedly in my eyes.

My heart was thumping, just like when I'd dreamed of my mom.

"It's important to remember that it's not something that actually happened, it's an allegory. Though of course it *could* happen," Mino said without emotion, just interpreting.

But I caught it. The shade of sadness hidden in the glint of Mino's eye.

"All right. You've made your point."

Chii, who had lifted herself up, collapsed heavily back into bed as if she no longer had the energy to sit up. She shut her eyes.

"I bet Paris will be wonderful for you," Mino said, himself again. "Maybe living there will be even nicer than it is here."

His return indicated that this session was over.

"How much?" I asked.

"Ten thousand yen," Mino said.

"That doesn't seem like much," I said, somewhat taken aback.

Judging from the atmosphere, I was sure it would be much more.

"We never accept more than that," Mino said.

I glanced over at Chii, planning to thank her, but her eyes were closed. Then, looking more closely, I noticed a photograph of their mother hanging on the wall behind her. I hadn't even seen it last time.

I could tell she was their mother by the shape of her body: she was kind of small and oddly proportioned, just like them. She stared straight out of the picture in its plain white frame.

It hit me that I recognized her. I had seen her on TV.

And suddenly I understood everything.

"Oh, my god, Mino! I didn't realize!"

He seemed to understand everything I wanted to say.

He nodded once.

I decided not to say anything more.

"I think I should go," I said, standing up.

As I left the room, a feeble, high-pitched voice called, "Good luck."

When I looked back, Chii was still asleep.

"I haven't heard her voice in a long time," Mino said. "I don't see why she has to use me if she can talk on her own."

"I bet she thinks you need a job, too," I said. "Besides, talking takes energy."

"I guess there's a reason for me to exist, after all," Mino said, smiling.

"What do mean, *a reason*! You matter very much to every-one!" I said earnestly.

Mino didn't reply.

His silence was exactly like Nakajima's, and it hurt to see him like that. He was quiet in the way people are when they believe the world would get along just fine without them.

I had one more cup of tea and then stepped outside. Mino brought out an empty plastic bottle and told me to take some spring water back for Nakajima.

Today, small waves rode the surface of the lake. There was a light breeze. The boats looked kind of lonely moored with no one sitting in them, rocking in time to the waves.

My mind felt numb, as if I were in an unreal world.

The tree branches were swaying slightly, too, hanging out over the lake. I noticed that they were cherry trees—lots and lots of them. I pictured the lake when they bloomed, framed by a ring of hazy, whitish pink.

"It must be lovely when the cherries are in bloom," I said.

"That's the most amazing event of the year here," Mino said.

He wasn't comfortable enough with me to come right out and invite me to visit then, but his manner made me feel as if he had.

Then we climbed the old stairway to the shrine, where the spring was.

Turning to look back when we reached the top, we were so high that the lake looked like an adorable miniature of itself, ensconced in a ring of greenery. The boats, lined up in a neat row, were like toy boats.

The spring water was cold and tasted slightly salty and hard when I scooped some up and drank it.

There was no one in the shrine; the only sound to be heard in the pure, cleanly swept space was the calling of birds.

It occurred to me that Nakajima and his mother had probably come here for water every day, too. I pictured the two of them then, living their lives, clinging to each other.

They were so hurt and they had lost so much that they no longer knew what was what, but the need they felt for each other was still love. No one could deny that.

Mino spoke. "Perhaps to your eyes, Chihiro, this lake looks like the kind of scenery you'd encounter in a dream—beautiful, ineffable.

"But that's because you saw it for the first time through Nobu's eyes.

"We have all kinds of days here, just like anywhere. The lake has all sorts of different faces. And so it's always fresh. Some days the sky is clear and the water shines so brightly you can't even look at it, and it lifts your spirit; some days it's plastered with boats. Sometimes I'll just sit staring at the snow melting away into nothing on the surface of the lake, and some days when it's overcast, even the trees in our garden look dingy. It'll be so hazy that our bicycles look like junk.

"The truth is, time hasn't really stopped for us. Things are constantly changing, even if the change happens so slowly you don't notice. I go to that big supermarket in front of the station and wander around looking like a kid, buying packages of curry rice mix with anime characters on them, collecting coupons. I buy things like buckets. Or a toilet brush. Ordinary stuff. And I cart it all home on my bike. You see that…" Mino pointed to a little general store that was visible a short distance from the lake. "That store over there. The man who runs it is part of our neighborhood association, so if we run into each other at the supermarket he gives me a lift in his car. His relatives are in Shizuoka, and in the winter they send him boxes of *mikan*. He brings us a lot, every year.

"But we don't get any friendlier with him than that.

"The priest at this shrine is a relative of Nobu's, but whenever we have business with him we just smile back and forth— we never have meals, or go out together. It's extremely rare for Chii and I to really grow close to someone. People are afraid of us, because we have a different sort of smell. And people scare us, too. But we're living our lives, just like everyone. We *live* in this place. Our lives may be warped, but we live them all the same. One day to the next."

"I know," I said. "And I'm sure that someday Nakajima

will realize that, too. That you're not just a part of his past. He was desperate to see you, even though it hurt him, even though it made him sick just thinking about coming here— but he had to find a way, right? That's how badly he wanted to see you. And he'll realize that if he feels that way, it's okay, he can come. I think he'll come visit more often now. Now that he's done it once, he'll be okay. You'll see more of Naka-jima. All the time, again and again."

Mino nodded without speaking.

Then he said, "I couldn't say it well earlier when you showed me the pictures, but ... thank you. Thanks for paint-ing us. Thanks so much for seeing, the first time you met us, that even though we're like ghosts, the two of us, even though we're not supposed to exist, we are alive."

I had seen Mino and Chii's mother on TV ages ago. She looked just like them.

She was notorious. People knew her as a terrible mother. She had joined a group that had done horrible things, and she had taken her children with her.

I don't remember them having a father. They had been born out of wedlock. Maybe their mother didn't know who the father was. The news was full of all kinds of scandalous reports about her back then. And if Mino and Chii's mother was presented as an incarnation of evil, Nakajima's mother was the incarnation of everything good.

Things are never that simple, and I don't see why it had to be reported that way.

I must have been in elementary school at the time.

If Nakajima had shown me a photograph of his mother instead of that wire rack, I'm sure I would have recognized her immediately. He probably knew that, and so he didn't.

Nakajima's mother was always pleading.

"Please return my son to me! I know he's alive. I'm his mother, I can tell!"

Every chance she had, she would be on TV, in magazines, on the radio, at rallies. She was always there, telling the same story. Telling people about the day her son was kidnapped.

Nakajima was a very bright child—too bright, in fact. He was a little different from other children. And so he would go and spend time at a special school. The school had a summer camp in Izu, and he had been going there, and then one evening he didn't come back. Until then, his mother explained, again and again, their family had been perfectly happy, and there was nothing at all unusual in their lives, nothing that wasn't as it should be.

Not long after that, the group began turning up in the news. It wasn't quite a religion: their goal was to live in accordance with certain principles, and create a new, ideal humanity. Naturally there was a sort of leader, and people gathered to listen to him preach, and then they established a commune deep in the mountains that was very nearly self-sufficient. That's the kind of group it was.

Reports about this organization circulated so widely that even someone like me, who never watched the news, knew its name, if little else. That's how notorious it was. After the kidnappings came to light, the group may have disbanded, or maybe it still lives on secretly in some form.

The truth is that in this world, things like that happen all the time. I heard all sorts of wild tales from all kinds of customers at my mom's club. Many were almost beyond belief; many had to do with what was, in essence, kidnapping.

Of course, on some level I'm hardly one to be held up as a paragon of normalcy. After all, before I turned ten, I started going to my mom's club and doing some of the stuff a hostess does, so I was raised in a pretty unconventional way. Sure, I was protected by my mom and dad, since their influence kept customers from trying anything funny with me, but if I'd wanted to explore different avenues, my environment would have made anything possible. No matter how high-class you aspire to be, in the entertainment business you're always trying to create a space where people can unload their irritations and frustrations, and I'm sure I must have been influenced

by that in some ways. That shadowy something is here inside me, just a little. The whiff of something purple in the
night, the sweet taste of darkness ... it's rubbed off on me, on
my body. Things were relatively okay at my mom's club because her customers weren't too bad, but even so I know just
how slimy people can be, and how people like that are during
the daytime. They don't get slimy at night because they're
drunk, they get slimy because they're already slimy to begin
with.

I remembered hearing people chatting at the club about that
incident, and watching reports on the TV there. Only it had
gotten all mixed up in my mind with other similar stories,
and I couldn't pick out any episodes in my memory that re-
lated specifically to Nakajima.

Nakajima's mother never, ever gave up. She would go on
every TV show and make herself available to every magazine,
doing missing-person shows and having psychics look for her
son, doing news programs, special features ... it's not an exag-
geration to say that there was never a day when you didn't see
her somewhere. She went on putting herself out there on a
regular basis, refusing to let people forget.

More than the event itself, she was what made the most
powerful impression. She always spoke extremely calmly,

only said what she was certain of, hardly ever shed a tear, and always looked straight ahead.

I could tell that until she found her son, nothing she ate would ever taste good, when she slept her dreams would always be nightmares, never light and easy, and no scenery would ever move her—she would just keep staring ahead into the distance, at her absent son. She would go on trying to connect.

Her endurance was astonishing. It was like she was reeling in a tiny, tiny thread, slender as a cobweb, which only occasionally caught the light, and she would never miss it when it did—that's how focused she was. It was love, and willpower. You could see it in her expression, as if it were painted there. She had this look on her face that told you all she could do was keep gazing at that one point, holding on to her faith, because if she ever so much as wondered if her son might be dead, then he really would die. Her face could have been the model for every mother in this world, or the face of a bodhisattva.

Then, finally, they found Nakajima. All the energy his mother had devoted to the search, distributing flyers all across the country, putting up photographs, going on TV until she was completely worn out—it had paid off.

A boy who had escaped from the group was picked up in a village at the foothills of a mountain. Someone who had seen Nakajima's mother on TV wondered if maybe this might be her son, and called the police.

It was such major news at the time, I can't understand why I didn't remember it, even just a little. I guess I never imagined it could have anything to do with my future.

Wow, that's awful, how terrible, I wonder what I'd do if it were me? I must have entertained these thoughts for about a second, and then they vanished. After all, I had a mom and dad, and my life was just beginning. It's amazing to realize how ignorant I was. And how innocent.

Things keep coming around and around in this world, it's all crammed violently together, two parts of the same skin. But I didn't realize that.

I doubt I'll ever understand how the three of them feel, no matter how long I live.

And ironically, it's that inability that puts them at ease.

So there's actually a reason for someone like *me* to exist in this world. Even before I start thinking about stuff like that, whether there is or isn't a reason, in some place that exists prior to such thoughts, an enormous wheel is spinning, and I'm caught up inescapably in its motion.

I'm its slave, almost. I'm free to think what I like, but it's all settled in advance.

Ever perceptive, Nakajima knew it as soon as he saw me that evening.

"Ah."

He must have sensed the turmoil in my heart as I stepped through the door.

Because that's what he said, the second I took my shoes off and looked up.

And then he tried to act like he didn't know, going on with his cleaning.

Nakajima was extraordinarily finicky what it came to keeping things neat, and he cleaned the apartment so frequently it made me feel kind of guilty. When I came home, everything would seem weirdly sterile—even the edges of the books were aligned. I couldn't help feeling that I'd drawn the winning number in this relationship. What's more, once he had started cleaning, he seemed unable to stop. Maybe that's what kept him going on this occasion, too. Either way, he went on quietly cleaning.

By then, I no longer felt like I could go on interacting with him the same way.

As long as it had remained a mystery, I could have dealt with it—no matter how enormous a mystery it became. Now that matters had gotten more specific, my imagination began supplying smells and textures.

There's a huge difference between "Something really, really terrible happened to me once" and "There was a period in my life when I was kidnapped and brainwashed."

Everything fell into place. The terror that physical contact inspired in him, his fear of seeing his friends from those days, his mother's seemingly unreasonable concern for him, his ability to cut his mind off from his body when he studied— all the delicious uncertainty was gone now, and in its place was a dank, oppressive weight.

You know, I told myself, *I'm not sure I can bear to hear the details—what his life there was actually like, why sex became so frightening to him. And maybe I'll never get over that.*

After a long time, I asked him, "Why did you say 'Ah' before?"

He stopped his cleaning, surprisingly, and looked at me.

And after that he was the same old Nakajima I knew and was crazy about, just as pathetic and as cool as always. The curly hair at the back of his neck, his slightly stooped posture, the way he went around the house so quietly—it was him, the same as ever. His palms, too, felt just as dry as they always had.

That set me at ease. We had a history here, together, in this apartment. That history was short, but it had nothing to do with his past.

It was so flimsy, a puff of air would send it flying, but it was real.

"I thought you'd figured something out," Nakajima said honestly. "Something about my past, I mean."

"How did you know?" I asked.

"Oh, it's happened with lots of people before—I can see it in people's eyes," Nakajima said. "And I was always on pins and needles about that, wondering when you'd realize. Of course, part of me wanted you to find out.... Do I disgust you now? Do you want to break up?"

I took Nakajima's hand in mine and pressed it so hard, so hard against my heart that I was probably about to break his bones.

"Don't say that," I said.

I used the sort of tone I might have used with a son.

And like a child Nakajima mumbled, "I'm sorry," and we went back to our lives.

I cooked dinner, and Nakajima continued cleaning. We worked in silence, like people the night before a move. Like we were starting life over again. Or like we had been doing this for a century already. Setting all kinds of things aside, willing to go back to the first days, if that's what it took, like Adam and Eve.

Nakajima's past would always be there, so the foundation could crumble at any moment. That's what happens, I realized, when people destroy other people.

We had finished eating when Nakajima spoke.

"Can we go see your mural?"

"If you want to. But I don't know—it's night. Wouldn't it be better to go in the daytime, when you can see better?"

"I'll go during the day, too, of course. I just thought we could go now, take a walk. I'm assuming it's finished, right?"

I figured we could go to see it whenever, so I hadn't actually told him it was done.

"All right, let's go," I said. "It's still early enough that the guard will let us in if I tell him I forgot something. He knows me by now. There's a street light near the wall, so I doubt it will be too dark to see anyway, but just in case we can take that giant flashlight."

The scents of spring hung over the dark street; the stars seemed hazy.

As we walked, Nakajima started talking.

"I was going to a summer camp run by this school I was going to, and somehow I got lost, I ended up deep in the mountains, wandering along the highway, and these people picked me up in their car, and that was it, I'd been kidnapped. This was long before cell phones, of course."

The story had begun.

The words kept coming, like water overflowing, refusing to stop.

He's like a broken machine, I thought.

Walking on, talking on, his arms folded over his chest.

All I could do was nod.

"Can you imagine what it's like to be kidnapped? Did it ever occur to you that you'd have to learn to *like* your kidnappers? Because that's the only way you can survive.

"Do you understand what that means?

"First, they erased my memory. With hypnotism and drugs. And they made me believe that the place we were in wasn't in Japan.

"I was a smart kid, so I knew how to resist the hypnotism. I had a vague memory of this technique I'd read about in a book, and I figured I'd try whatever I could, and somehow I managed to make it work.

"What you had to do was practice a kind of autosuggestion, you make yourself remember a given person whenever you see a particular object, and since I was in Izu I knew the ocean had to be somewhere nearby, so I hypnotized myself into remembering my mother whenever I saw the ocean or if I found myself standing on the shore. After that I just let them do what they wanted with me. It was scary, but in the end it worked.

"Several months later, when we went down to the beach one very cold night for meditation practice, I remembered my mom. It took a few days after that for me to recall that we were in Japan, and to think I might have been kidnapped. There were a number of families in the group, parents and children both, like Mino and Chii and their mother, and I had gotten so used to it being that way that I almost took it for granted. Their mother wasn't living in the same room as them—the group had some ideological reason for that—but they put us together, and we all slept in a row. Holding hands, like the three strokes of the character for 'river.'

"During the daytime, teachers in different fields would come and lead discussions and study groups and stuff. For kids and adults both.

"At first after I remembered I got so confused I thought I was going crazy, but I waited a few days without letting on about anything, and little by little I started analyzing the situation I was in. I came up with a hypothesis about what must have happened, the thing that seemed closest to the truth, and in the end I made up my mind to escape.

"It wouldn't have been a surprise if I'd gone crazy then.

"I had to go wild inside myself, fighting to keep my sanity.

"People try instinctively to take the easy route, right? We shy away from pain.

"So I didn't want to believe that the people I was living with then, day after day, were bad, and my mind would drift off on its own, trying to think that the things I had remembered were fake, that *they* were the lie. I hated the thought of leaving Mino and Chii, there was no ambiguity in that, and it frightened me to think of what might happen to them if I escaped and the police came. At times like that, your thoughts are inevitably drawn to the worst-case scenario.

"Is this really a foreign country? No, it has to be Japan. But I was born here, I grew up in this place. No, that's not true. I was kidnapped. Kidnapping is bad—I've got to do something. But they're all such good people, how could I accuse them of something like that? How long have I been here? Has it been a really long time? I wonder if Mom is still alive . . . I was bewildered. *Is this woman I keep remembering my mom? No, I know she isn't, she's just a vision I created because I want a mom so badly . . .* Everything got tangled up like that, the thoughts kept hounding me. I don't say that lightly: my mind was really being torn to pieces, stripped of everything inside it, and I started getting very unstable.

"So finally I got up the courage to talk with Mino and Chii.

"And this is what Mino said, late at night, in a whisper:

"'I think you're probably right, Nobu. I've been living here with everyone ever since I was a baby, so I don't really know about certain things, but I think you were probably stolen. I mean, it's odd that your mom isn't here. And this *is* Japan. That's for sure. Even though everyone says it isn't.'

"He had no idea how it might affect him and his sister, but still he told me his opinion. In a sense, he was risking his life, and I can't ever be grateful enough to him for that, as long as I live. Even though it is so hard for me to go and see them.

"The reason Chii is bedridden, and the reason I get so exhausted sometimes—it's not just a matter of emotional trauma. All the drugs they gave us destroyed our livers. Mino has gotten a lot better, but I don't think he's completely recovered, either.

"Not long after the group disbanded, Mino and Chii's mother died of liver cancer.

"The house they live in now was originally used as a kind of combined storage and meeting room for the shrine, and that's why my mother and I were able to live there a while, and when Mino and Chii's mother died we decided to invite them to live there, without paying any rent or anything. We wanted them to feel free to stay there forever. After all, part of me still isn't sure whether what I did was really best for them. Maybe they would have been better off if I hadn't informed on the group when I escaped, and they could have just stayed there like that for the rest of their lives. Sometimes I wonder. So I wanted to find a way to help them out with their new lives, and to protect them from society. My mom felt exactly the same way."

Nakajima's arms remained tightly folded across his chest. I knew the street we were walking on very well, and yet it seemed somehow to be detached from the earth, subtly distorted.

Plodding on with even steps, I listened.

"The group hadn't been living in that place all along—evidently they were moving around from place to place, all over Japan, looking for somewhere to settle. So all kinds of people were coming and going all the time. It wasn't at all unusual to suddenly see some face you didn't recognize, or for someone who had been there to disappear, so it wasn't hard for me to escape.

"The thought that scared me the most was that maybe I'd keep going and going, but maybe I'd never arrive anywhere, and if I finally came to a populated area I'd find that it really was a foreign country, and I wouldn't be able to communicate, and it would turn out that all those memories I'd had really were just an illusion. I didn't have a passport, so I would have no way of getting back to the 'home' I was thinking of anyway. So I'd just have to go back to the same place and live there again. Without any hope. What if *that* turned out to be the truth? These thoughts plagued me endlessly. That was the worst, it really was.

"I started thinking that if that were the case, I'd rather just be dead.

"If this little dream I'd cherished turned out not to be there for me to hold on to anymore, I mean. Because it wasn't just my mother I was dreaming of. It was the background against which I came into this world, the scent of freedom that wafted through my life, supported by all the hopes and the love my parents had for me, because back then, when I was still a kid, things like that were everything to me.

"My head was spinning, and the world before me looked so dark, I was ready to lie down right there on the spot and die.

"But I had Mino. His words, etched deep in my mind, were my reality then.

"I could count on Mino. I'm sure I would have despaired even more if he hadn't told me we were in Japan, probably in a place called Shimoda, even though no one ever said so.

"He had been growing suspicious for some time as a result of information he got from his mysterious sister. He was secretly afraid that the adults might learn about her strange powers, and then their mother would end up in an even stronger position in the group, and they would have to stay even longer than they might otherwise. He tried his best to hide the things she said from them, but it was really hard. So I had no choice but to save them. I don't know if they would agree that what I did deserves to be called 'saving,' though. After all, both their parents were part of the group—at least I'm pretty sure their father was, too. I'm sure their wounds, the despair they felt, must have been a lot deeper than mine.

"I think what Mino did for me, his noble sacrifice, destroyed any sense of stability he'd had. And Chii's, too. And even if that stability was built on a lie, at the time it was still something they could rely on. After that, everything changed. And yet he wanted that change, although maybe he wanted it for us, in order to save me and Chii—and that act of love, more than anything, is the reason he can keep smiling the way he does, even now.

"I trudged through the forest, thinking only of Mino's words, and of my mother.

"I get the sense that most people assume that when someone who's been brainwashed comes out of it there's a feeling of relief, that it's like waking up, but it isn't like that. You feel sort of dull, nothing is clear—it makes you miserable. That's the truth. I felt like there was nothing good waiting for me. I would actually keep feeling that way for a long time. Right then, though, making my way along that dark mountain road, I wasn't worried about that, I was just fighting for my life. Trying to keep from getting torn to pieces inside, trying to hold myself together.

"Eventually I saw lights, and my heart started thumping, my head hurt so badly it felt like it was about to split, and all the scary stories I had ever heard weighed down on me until I could hardly bear it anymore. But I kept walking. I stepped, almost collapsed, into the light. I didn't know what it was, but there was a fence around the space, and I had the sensation of something beautiful watching me, so I stumbled over in that direction, and there was a stable with five horses lined up in their stalls, looking out at me.

"For some reason the horses didn't get nervous or start acting up when they saw me; they simply stood there watching me, perfectly still. Their black eyes and their lustrous coats made me feel completely calm. I stretched out a hand and touched one of them. I wasn't afraid he would bite me. I just wanted to touch him, because he was so lovely. His skin felt warm, and then I caught a whiff of animal smell, and I loved the hard feel of his coat, stiff like grass—my eyes filled with tears. The horse just kept looking at me, it didn't seem to be thinking anything, his eyes were like two lakes, so gorgeous, drawing me in.

"I'll be grateful to that horse for the rest of my life.

"That horse, with its wild, natural eyes, brought me back, made me all right.

"I pulled myself together again, got a grip.... The place I was in, it was a small riding club. I went and knocked on the clubhouse door. People who had come in from riding and the couple who owned the club were inside chatting over coffee, and they were pretty taken aback when they saw me, but the wife seemed to deduce immediately from how I looked that something was very wrong. She told me to come inside and sat me down at the back of the room and made me some coffee. The coffee smelled good, but even better than that was her smell—she smelled like a mother. The kind of bodily, nice scent of a mother who never lets her children out of her sight, who always thinks first of her kids—I smelled it. And it brought back such memories, it was so warm and familiar, that I cried and cried and couldn't stop.

"'You're Japanese, right? So this is Japan, after all? Please, call the police. I don't even know my own name right now, honest. I was kidnapped.'

"I kept repeating those words, crying all the while.

"And then one of the riders said he recognized me, he had seen my mother on TV, and so right away the woman's husband called the police.

"'You can tell us the details later', the woman said, and gave me more coffee and some curry rice. There was lots of meat in it, and I realized how much I had missed that, too. When I was with that group, we weren't allowed to eat any meat at all.

"And it came back to me that this is what a mother is, this is the kind of being she is—it doesn't matter what the situation is, if someone's cold she warms him, and if he's hungry she wants to feed him. I remembered that with such intensity, so vividly. It was okay for me to remember now, I realized, and I wanted to cry, but I couldn't cry anymore. It took time for my heart to unclench itself."

We arrived at the center. Nakajima stopped talking while I chatted with the guard.

Then, as we walked through the small gate, I asked my first question.

"And you and your mom went to live in that house by the lake after you got back?"

Nakajima nodded. After that, he started speaking again, but less rapidly.

"I was almost ten at the time, but after I returned my mother and I slept in the same futon every night, with her hugging me tight. And for about three months, every morning when we woke up she would look at my face and burst out sobbing. I remember the suffocating feeling I got, even when my eyes were closed—the sense that someone is staring at you, at your face. I knew if I opened my eyes I'd see her, her face swollen from crying, so I just lay there, pretending to be asleep. It felt so oppressive, I'm sure it was even worse than what you feel being with me now, dealing with the things you don't know about me. It was so over the top that my father got fed up and left her. That's how bad it was." Nakajima smiled. "I worried that she might go crazy, and so I asked if she could join me for counseling, even though it was really only meant for me, and we did go together, for a long time. Even then, with her in that condition, she did whatever was necessary to protect me when the media came to do a story on us, and she told me we were going to make up for the time I'd lost— sometimes we'd go places, amusement parks and so on, and my father would come along, too.

"Apparently my face was expressionless in the beginning, no matter what we were doing, I was always stiff, but that was just because I couldn't find a way to show what I was feeling. Inside, I was having all kinds of emotions, but it was impossible to let them out. But day by day, slowly, over time, something was warming up in me, thawing. I started to love my mother again, and gradually I went back to being myself. I remember it all very clearly, that whole process.

"And then, after things had settled down somewhat, our doctor suggested that we should go take it easy somewhere, and we went and lived in that house, by the edge of the lake."

That explains why he's like this, I thought. It's because he experienced something so awful himself that he's determined, more than most people, not to be a burden to anyone, to me, and to take care of himself.

Nakajima continued.

"It's not like I was being abused the whole time or anything, I was simply being trained by people who wanted to create a race of superhumans, so in a sense they were all very nice, the meals were always good, with lots of seafood, and I had friends I could play with every day, so it was actually pretty fun. But as far as the adults there were concerned, my relationships with them were all the same, homogeneous, there was no emotional involvement like there had been in my relationship with my mother.

"I realized then, in the most physical way, that being logical and clear-headed isn't at all the same thing as having everything the same, unruffled. When you're in a state of homogeneity, it means you've lost yourself. That's how you're able to get that way in the first place.

"All that love my mother sort of forced on me right after I escaped, it was like a soup that was too strong, it penetrated too deep. Her emotions were so intense—they were like gaudy clothes or something, with too many frills. That's how I saw it.

"In the end, I think it was my fault my mother and father separated, and she died sooner than she should have. That seemed to me like the most natural thing in the world, and I'm not thinking in some weird unscientific way or anything. It happened because she used so much energy; she chose to do that, in return for getting me back. What she put into me was taken away from her. She knew it would be like that, and still she used that energy. I really believe that, even now.

"Of course, I don't necessarily feel like I have that long to live myself, and so back then it was natural for me to think, *What are you doing, I don't need this life, Mom, it's yours!* But I didn't have the strength to pray for that to happen, really deep down, the way my mother did. I could never compete with her, I realized that. She gave it everything she had, squeezing every last drop of strength in her body into following the tiny thread that led her to me.

"I've been broken in all kinds of ways, and so for a long time now I've had the sense that I won't be able to make it through my life in a normal way. But thanks to my mother, somehow or other I've been able to balance the books, and things have turned out really well.

"Except it still makes me feel a little sad to think that the whole time she was searching for me, wearing herself out, I was having sashimi and laughing with my friends, and getting my first taste of the joys of sex," Nakajima said.

"Sorry, I cry when I talk about all this," he added. And then he really cried.

Nakajima and his mother had spent every day together, like lovers, trying to reclaim their lost time, and that ended up being the best period of his life, and providing his most precious memories. I doubted anything better than that would ever happen to him. He lived knowing that he had already experienced perfection; that, no doubt, was what gave him a certain aura of sadness, and a sense of flexibility.

"Emotions aren't much, though. I understand that quite well. Just as my memories of living with my mother by the lake are the most precious I have now, in the days after I started living with her I was always thinking of the ocean, how much fun I'd always had there, playing with Mino and Chii.... The waves were always rough at Shimoda, and we would see each other one second, and then the next we'd lose sight of each other. We'd laugh our heads off for no reason, fall down, get sucked in by the waves, and play so hard that we got out of breath.

"When I try to gather up all the *good things*, I get an infinite number of combinations of events that fall under that heading, and if I try to gather up the *painful things*, those memories start coming out, and either way they'll just keep coming, called up out of my brain or my heart or whatever, and none of it really means very much.

"Just because things turned out badly in the end doesn't mean that anything has changed in my relationship with my mother. Everything is still there, the same as always: the fact that we walked slowly around that lake together, holding hands, and the way my friends and I laughed in the ocean, the fact that I was looking at a seagull then. None of it has changed. It's neither good nor bad, as I see it, the scenes are just there inside me, forever, and their mass remains the same. Of course, it's true that sometimes the pink at sunrise somehow seems brighter than the pink at sunset, and that when you're feeling down the landscape seems darker, too—you see things through the filter of your own sensibility. But the things themselves, out there, they don't change. They existed, and that's all there is to it.

"Maybe it's not even accurate to say things turned out badly. Sure, an accumulation of little incidents ended up ripping my life to shreds, and my mother swept all those pieces up with her too-passionate hands and jammed them together again any which way. That turned me into a kind of patchy guy. But I have my life, I'm living it. It's twisted, exhausting, uncertain, and full of guilt, but nonetheless, there's something there. And that something is always greater than these emotions of mine."

Nakajima sounded, the way he murmured these words, as if he had only grudgingly decided to speak them.

It was easy for me to listen, since I'd never been broken like him. That's how people are, pretty much, wherever in the world you might go. There's no need to forgive every mistake, to learn to like the bad things, we tell ourselves, and so we forgive just enough, in an easy sort of way.

Take my mom, for instance. She was clumsy and terrible at math, she was nothing but a Mama-san at a bar, she had tons of plastic surgery, she died young, she had a child out of wedlock. Or my totally uncool dad, acting like a dipstick in that cheesy Italian restaurant. You need to have all that stuff, because that's where it all begins.

I'm sure it's even harder for Nakajima. Because the scale is so huge.

But who knows, maybe if he can get used to the fact that each day is another dull repetition of the same old thing, being with the same people all the time, nothing but the little leaps of your heart to put a splash of color in the world ... if he can get accustomed to that, maybe, little by little, something will start to change.

Not only was the street light shining on the wall, but the nearly full moon was shining pretty brightly, too—we could see the mural fairly well even from a distance. Certainly the colors would have shown up better in the daytime, but there was a kind of mysterious air to it, the way the outermost edges faded off into the darkness.

"See, I painted everyone in over here," I said, with a certain amount of pride.

"Wow, so this is what it's like." Nakajima gazed at the mural for a long time, which was nice. It made me happy to see the same expression on his face that he gets when he's studying really hard.

I felt how important the simplest things were, like feeling proud, finding something funny, stretching yourself, retreating into yourself.

Clearly I was recovering, too, from all kinds of things.

I wanted to get back on my own two feet first, and then lead him by the hand down the path we would take together. Like the first time we went to see Mino and Chii, drawing instinctively closer to him, without any hidden motives.

Gazing all the while at the picture, very slowly, I explained. My voice reverberated through the dark, empty yard.

"This is you. You're taking it easy in the shade of the tree, eating a banana. And this is your mother—she's always hovering around you, smiling. And here's the lake, and obviously this is the shrine. And then over here, this is Mino. He's laughing, making tea. See how small he is? And Chii, sleeping in her canopied bed. A little monkey princess. No one else knows what it means, but that doesn't matter—it's a happy world. No one can destroy that happiness. People will see this wall without having any idea what it means, and then eventually it will be knocked down, and it won't exist anymore. But deep down in people's subconscious, this happy group of monkeys, all of you, will still be there, just a little. Isn't that nice?"

Nakajima nodded without speaking.

"Lately I'm always crying," he said then, snuffling a bit, so I didn't look at him. *What the hell?* I was thinking, a bit ruefully. *This isn't love, it's volunteer work. This should be the scene where the guy is moved and embraces the girl, right? C'mon!*

We stood there looking at the wall for ages, so long we started getting cold.

Whenever I think of this mural in the future, I'll remember this night.

No matter where we may be, or what we're doing.

"I don't really know how to ask this, Chihiro, but did they … did they look unhappy to you?"

Nakajima had been walking in silence when he blurted this out, his voice hoarse.

I thought hard.

I had the feeling that if I lied now, everything would turn into a lie.

There's the surface, and then what we see under the surface. Delicious tea, a dusty room, the lake glittering outside the window…

I tried my best to bring it all together into a single impression, layer upon layer, like a slice of mille-feuille. And then I answered.

"They didn't seem unhappy to me. Not at all," I said. "They didn't seem especially happy, either. They looked like they must have unhappy moments, and happy moments, too."

"I'm glad." Nakajima seemed relieved.

Talking with him could be like a battle of wills, but I didn't mind.

In fact, I kind of liked it.

"You know, Chihiro, it's true. You're really extremely unusual," Nakajima said. "You don't use emotional violence against people, or hardly ever anyway."

"That's not true," I said. "I've got scary sides, too, I'm sure. Everyone does."

"I'm not saying you don't have any. I'm just saying you've got less of that. And that's good enough for me. I was afraid of losing you, so I didn't want to get too close. But that didn't matter, you were still there every day, in your own world, free from worries about other people. There's nothing uncertain about you, out there painting, moving your hands and your body, and I feel so at ease because of that. Except that you're *so* optimistic—that kind of worries me. I get afraid, because I can't trust that. But I'm drawn to you. Sometimes I feel this urge to just go ahead and mess all this up, but I can't, because I love you."

Nakajima smiled, just a little.

"It's great you can talk like that now, isn't it? That's progress," I said truthfully.

"Hmph. I'm not going to Paris with you if you're going to be like that," he said, sounding like a child.

"All right." I laughed. "Why don't you go by yourself, then?"

"That's fine with me. I'll go all alone, and I'll be waiting. I've been thinking, though—sometime do you think you'd come to Shimoda with me? I'd like to go visit that place eventually, and go to that riding club and say thank you to the people there, and above all to the horses. It would still be too hard for me to do that now, though. There's no way, it'd be totally impossible."

"Why don't we go when we come back from Paris for a visit, then, just make it part of the trip? We could go swimming together if we go in the summer."

Nakajima and I ambled off through the familiar neighborhood, just like always, chatting back and forth—not in a particularly happy way, but not in a sad way, either. There was a real sense of comfort, and yet at the same time it felt oddly tense. The feeling that every little thing we said, these conversations, at any moment they could stop being possible, and so they were precious, it was that feeling, and the sense of the miracle of this shared moment, here and now.

Why were we so far apart, even when we were together?

It was a nice loneliness, like the sensation of washing your face in cold water.

"But before we do that," I said, "let's go back to the lake, to see Mino and Chii. Let's go see the lake when the cherry trees are in bloom, all around it."

"You'd go again? Really?" Nakajima said.

"If we go enough, maybe things will be all right," I said. "All kinds of things."

Here we were, two ridiculously fragile people, sliding along on a very thin layer of ice all the time, each of us ready to slip and take the other down at any moment, the most unsteady of couples—and yet I believed what I had said. It would be all right.

Going along like that, I felt like we were high above the clouds, shining.

"I'm sure they'd like that, too," Nakajima said.

"Maybe someday I'll even be able to see Chii when she's better, up and about."

That was unlikely, of course, but there's nothing wrong with being a little hopeful. Who says you can't warm your frozen limbs in the faint heat of a flicker of hope?

"For the time being, let's go back home and I'll make us some tea with some really good water," I said. "Even if it won't be as delicious as Mino's."